Special Delivery

Special Delivery

Ann M. Martin

SCHOLASTIC INC.

NEW YORK ◇ TORONTO ◇ LONDON ◇ AUCKLAND
SYDNEY ◇ MEXICO CITY ◇ NEW DELHI ◇ HONG KONG

ISBN-13: 978-0-545-06895-6
ISBN-10: 0-545-06895-9

12 11 10 9 8 7 6 5 4 3 2 1   9 10 11 12 13 14/0

Printed in the U.S.A.

First printing, October 2009

The author would like to congratulate Matalyn Lund, winner of the 2007 Main Street Contest and creator of Maty's Magic Store, the newest business on Main Street.

Camden Falls

1 *The Morris Family*

2 *The Hamilton Family*

3 *The Malone Family*

4 *Min, Flora, and Ruby*

5 *Olivia Walter and her family*

6 *Mr. Pennington*

7 *Robby Edwards and his parents*

8 *The Fong Family*

CHAPTER I

Sunday Morning, November 22nd

Flora Marie Northrop lay in her cozy bed in her cozy home in Camden Falls, Massachusetts, and reflected that there was nothing quite like a Sunday morning. Except maybe for a Saturday morning, but Flora's Saturday had been busy. She and her sister and their friends had spent much of the day at Bingham Mall (without adults — the first time for all four of them), and she had gotten out of bed early that morning in a great rush of excitement. Now, on Sunday, she lay contentedly under her comforter, wriggling her toes in the delicious warmth, her hand caressing her cat, King Comma, who had crawled under the covers sometime during the night and hadn't stirred since.

Flora yawned mightily. She lifted the covers and peered in at King. "I'm surprised you aren't meowing for your breakfast," she said to him. But then she squinted at her clock and saw that it was only seven-thirty — which was why she was very surprised to hear the doorbell ring just a few moments later. "Who on earth could that be?" she asked aloud. She raised her shade and looked out onto the front lawn. She couldn't see who might be standing on the stoop below, but she thought that the car parked in front of her house belonged to Aunt Allie.

Curious, Flora slid out of bed, leaving King purring in his snug cave, and hurried out of her room. She met her grandmother Min in the hallway. Min was tying the sash of her ancient bathrobe and trying to pat her hair in place at the same time.

"It's Aunt Allie," said Flora. "At least, I think it's her car parked in the street."

"Goodness me," said Min. "I hope nothing's wrong."

Flora was certain her grandmother was remembering the night nearly two years earlier when she had received a phone call from the police saying that Flora and her sister, Ruby, and their parents had been in a car accident, and that Mr. and Mrs. Northrop had died. One phone call, one ring of the doorbell, and lives could be changed in unthinkable ways.

Flora rushed ahead of Min down the stairs, but Min said, "Let me answer the door," and peeked cautiously through the front window. "My stars and garters, it *is* Allie," she said. She flung open the door. "Allie? What's the matter? Has something happened?"

Flora could tell from the smile — no, the grin — on her aunt's face that nothing was the matter, and that whatever had happened was very good.

Allie closed the door in a hurry, but a gust of cold air burst inside anyway, and Flora shivered. "I'm sorry," said Allie. "I'm sorry to come over so early, but I waited as long as I could —" She stopped suddenly, put her hand to her mouth as if she might begin to sob, and then grinned again. She drew in a breath. "Is Ruby up yet? I have something important to say, and I want to say it to all of you at once."

Flora, now dying of curiosity, hurled herself up the stairs, calling over her shoulder, "I don't know if she's awake yet, but I'll get her." She left her aunt and her grandmother behind, Allie shrugging out of her heavy coat, and Min saying, "I'll put on a pot of coffee."

Flora knocked on Ruby's door, waited less than a second for an answer (which was not forthcoming), and then threw the door open. "Ruby!" she cried.

Still no answer.

"Ruby Jane!"

"I'm sleeping," said Ruby from beneath her own comforter.

"No, you're not. You're talking to me. You have to come downstairs right now. Aunt Allie is here and she says she has something important to tell us." When Ruby said nothing, Flora added, "It's a big mystery."

"What time is it?" muttered Ruby.

"Seven-thirty-three," Flora replied instantly.

"That's too early."

"That's what makes this a mystery. Come *on*. First Aunt Allie was smiling, then she almost cried, and then she started smiling again. Something's going on. And she won't tell us what it is until we're all there."

"That's blackmail," said Ruby.

"Maybe she won the lottery," suggested Flora.

Ruby flung her covers back. "Huh. And she wants to share her winnings with us. Okay." She found a sweatshirt swirled in a mound of clothes at the foot of her bed and pulled it on over her nightgown. "We do have interesting lives. First we became orphans, now we're going to be rich orphans."

"I hardly think —" Flora began to say, and then stopped. Arguing with Ruby was usually pointless, just one of the many ways in which she and her sister were different. Ruby, ten years old and in fifth grade at Camden Falls Elementary, was stubborn and talkative and overly confident. Her life revolved around performing — singing, acting, and dancing (she was a triple threat, she had once told Flora with great assurance) — and she liked nothing better than being the center of attention. Flora, twelve and a seventh-grader at Camden Falls Central High School, was quiet, shy, craved time spent alone in her room, lived in fear of being the center of attention, and engaged in activities that were as quiet as she was — sewing, knitting, reading, and attending to her homework. Flora was responsible and studious and usually at the top of her class. Ruby was impulsive and hasty and paid little attention to her grades. She gave Min a run for her money. (Flora had overheard her grandmother say this to Allie one day, which had made Flora even more aware of all that Min had given up in order to take care of her daughter's daughters, more aware of everything that had changed in Min's life as well as in Flora's and Ruby's in the last two years.)

"Hey, space cadet!" called Ruby rudely from her doorway. "I thought you said Aunt Allie won't tell us whatever it is until we're all downstairs. Let's get going."

Flora shook herself from her thoughts and followed her sister to the living room. Min and Allie were sitting side by side on the couch, Daisy Dear stretched languidly between them, her big doggie head in Min's lap, her rump in Allie's lap. Flora could smell coffee brewing.

"Oh!" said Allie when she caught sight of the girls, and Flora had the feeling once again that her aunt might start to cry. "Ruby, thank you for getting up early, honey. I have something to tell you, all three of you. I wanted to tell you last night, but" (Allie turned to her mother) "I knew you were out with Rudy Pennington."

Flora tried hard not to scowl. Exactly how often did her grandmother plan to go out on dates with Mr. Pennington? So much dating at their advanced age was unseemly.

Allie folded her hands in her lap. "I have big news," she announced.

"Yes." Ruby nodded solemnly. "The lottery. We know."

Allie looked puzzled, and Flora elbowed her sister, then pulled her down until they were squished together in an armchair. Aunt Allie clasped and unclasped her hands, looked in turn at Min, at Ruby, at Flora, and finally said, "I'm going to be a mother."

"What?" said Flora and Ruby.

"*What?!*" cried Min with such fervor that she levitated from the couch, dislodging Daisy's head.

"I thought you were supposed to be married if you were going to have a baby," added Ruby.

And Flora thought, but was too polite to say, that her aunt — her mother's sister who had never, ever been married — was too old to get pregnant in any case.

"No, no," said Allie quickly. "I mean I'm going to *adopt* a baby. I just found out that one is about to be born and I've been chosen to be the adoptive mom."

"But," said Min, who had plopped back onto the couch, "how did this happen? This is so sudden. You never said anything . . ." Her voice trailed off.

Allie sighed. "I know. It's silly, but I was afraid if I told anyone what I was doing I'd jinx things and then I would never get a call like the one I got last night. It was from a woman — her name is Mrs. Prescott — at one of the agencies I registered with."

"*One* of the agencies?" repeated Min.

"I've been looking for a long time," said Allie. "I want to be a mom — it's almost all I can think about — and then last night, out of the blue, Mrs. Prescott called and said that there's a young mom, a *very* young mom, in New York City, who's about to give birth to her baby prematurely, and she and the father have decided they can't keep the baby. They're still in school, they don't earn any money. . . . Anyway, after the baby is born, he —"

"It's a boy?" squealed Ruby.

"I mean, he or she," amended Allie. "He or she will come home with me."

There was a moment of stillness in the living room, and then Flora shot to her feet and began jumping up and down. She grabbed Ruby's arms, and they danced back and forth in front of the couch until Daisy let out a bark of alarm. Min leaned over and hugged Allie. "I'm going to be a grandmother again," she said into Allie's ear, tears starting to fall.

"And we're going to have a cousin!" exclaimed Flora. "Oh, this is the best, best day ever!"

"But, Allie, please, you have to give us details," said Min, disengaging herself from her daughter. "Forgive me if I sound shocked. It's just that this is the first we've heard of any of this."

"I know, I know." Allie smiled at her dancing nieces, who now fell, laughing, into the armchair. "Well, I suppose it began —"

"Wait," said Min, "let me get our coffee." She left the living room and returned a few minutes later carrying a tray holding two cups of coffee and two glasses of orange juice.

"Okay," said Ruby, reaching for a glass of juice. "Start over." (She was mildly annoyed that she was not going to be able to march into school the next day and tell her class that she had, overnight, become rich.)

"It began," said Aunt Allie again, "a few years ago when I was living in New York City and seeing a man named Paul Maulden. We were very serious about each other and planned to get married. Then, after lots of doctor's appointments, I found out that I can't have children. Paul and I were terribly disappointed, but we decided that we wanted to adopt a child, and because adoption can take a long time, we thought we should get things started right away, even before we got married. First we considered adopting a baby girl from China" (at this, Flora and Ruby exchanged a glance, remembering the mysterious closet stocked with baby things — mostly baby *girl* things — that they had come across in Aunt Allie's house one evening) "so we filled out an application. Then we filled out applications with several other agencies. And then . . ."

Allie's voice faltered, and Flora found herself silently chanting, "Please don't let her cry, please don't let her cry."

"And then," Allie continued, sounding stronger, "a year ago, Paul ended our relationship. He said it just wasn't going to work. And that's why I decided to move back here. I wanted a change."

"*Oh*. That explains things," said Ruby sagely.

"But I never gave up my dream of having a child. I want to be a mother *very* badly. In fact, the closer I've gotten to you two," Allie went on, glancing at her nieces, "the more that desire grew. So I continued filling out forms and applications and signing on with agencies to adopt as a single parent. I've just been waiting for the moment when *some*thing would come through. And last night it happened. The phone rang and it was Mrs. Prescott telling me about this baby."

"And the baby is definitely going to be yours?" asked Flora.

"Well, almost definitely. A mandatory waiting period follows the birth, during which one or both of the parents could decide to keep the baby after all. But it doesn't sound as though that's going to happen. The bigger question is when the baby will be born. The mother went to the hospital yesterday in early labor, but the doctors want to try to delay the birth for at least several weeks. The longer they can delay it, the healthier the baby will be."

"I see," said Min.

"And so," said Aunt Allie, "I don't know *when* the baby will be born. It could happen now or it could happen in a month. But . . . I've decided to go to New York City for a week. Do you remember my friends Debbie and David?" she asked Min.

"The ones who live in Greenwich Village?"

Allie nodded. "They're going to be away this week, and a month or so ago they had offered me the use of their apartment while they were out of town. They thought I might want to spend Thanksgiving in the city. I said no, because I wanted to be here with you, but now I've decided to take them up on their offer. I spoke to them last night and they said of course I could still stay in their apartment. So I'm going to drive to New York this afternoon and stay until next Sunday. After all, there's a *slight* chance the baby might be born in the next few days, and if that happens, I want to be close at hand."

"You get to go to New York City?" cried Ruby, and Flora couldn't tell whether Ruby was excited or jealous. Furthermore, she seemed to be entirely missing the point about the baby.

"Ruby, she used to *live* in New York," said Flora. "And anyway, she's going back there to get her baby. Maybe."

"I know," said Ruby, who pouted so dramatically that Flora could tell it was her stage pout and not a natural one.

"Aunt Allie, when will you get to bring the baby home?" asked Flora, hoping that Ruby would notice that *this* was an appropriate and not self-centered question.

"Not until after the waiting period is over *and* the baby is healthy enough to leave the hospital. It could be a while. That's why I know it's silly to rush down to the city. But you never know what might happen. And I was planning to take this week off anyway, so I might as well make the trip." Allie paused. "I'll have to call Mr. Willet and tell him I can't come to his Thanksgiving dinner. I feel bad about that."

"He'll understand, honey," said Min.

Flora envisioned their former neighbor Mr. Willet, who had recently moved out of the Row Houses, where Flora and Ruby lived with Min. Flora's house was the fourth from the left in the row of attached homes. Mr. Willet and his wife had lived in the second house from the left. But after Mrs. Willet had developed Alzheimer's disease, Mr. Willet found a place for her at Three Oaks, a nearby retirement community, and soon followed her there himself. Thanksgiving was to be his first holiday away from the familiar Row Houses, and he had invited Aunt Allie, Min, Flora, Ruby, and Mr. Pennington (who lived in the third Row House from the right) to join him for Thanksgiving dinner in the dining room at Three Oaks. Flora was very much looking forward to the holiday.

"Wow," said Ruby, "this is going to be some week. I mean, there's the baby and the holiday — and, of course, my solos in the Thanksgiving concert on Thursday morning. By the way, did I mention that I'm going to have the *main* solo next month in the Christmas concert?"

"Only about a thousand times," muttered Flora.

"Well, I think I can make this week even more exciting," said Min.

Three heads swiveled toward her.

"How?" asked Ruby.

"Allie, what would you say to our joining you in New York for a few days? We could take the train down on Friday morning and stay with you until Sunday. There's room at Debbie and David's, isn't there?"

"Sure," said Allie, a smile creeping across her face. "Oh, that would be wonderful!"

"Wonderful?! It would be stupendous!" shrieked Ruby, who leaped out of the chair and began dancing around the living room again. "'New York! New York!'" she sang. "'A fabulous town! The Bronx is up and the Battery's down!' Whatever that means. Oh, this is going to be so cool. Can we go to the Empire State Building? Can we see a show on Broadway? Can we —"

"Ruby," said Min, "please calm down. We will do as much as we can, but remember that since I'm planning the trip at rather a late date, we might not be able to do everything you want."

"Okay, okay. I don't care. As long as we get to go to the Great Big Old Apple."

Flora's mind was on other things. "Min, we'll have a baby to sew for! Our very own baby! I'm going to start smocking right away. Aunt Allie, is there any way you could find out whether the baby is a boy or a girl? Oh, it doesn't matter. I can just start sewing."

"And I'll start knitting," said Min. "We got a wonderful new book of baby patterns in at the store. Oh, the store! I'll have to ask Gigi if she can cover for me next weekend." (Min and her friend Gigi, grandmother to Flora's best friend, Olivia, ran a sewing and needlework store on Main Street called Needle and Thread.)

"I'd better get going," said Allie, rising to her feet. "I have to pack for the week."

"For the love of Mike," said Min. "A baby on the way."

"A trip to New York City," said Ruby.

"A new cousin," said Flora.

"And all before eight-thirty in the morning," added Min, looking at her watch.

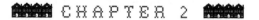

CHAPTER 2

Sunday Afternoon, November 22nd

After Aunt Allie left, Ruby looked at her own watch. "It *is* only eight-thirty," she said in surprise. "It feels much, much later."

"That's because you usually lie around in bed until ten on the weekends," said Flora.

Ruby put her hands on her hips. "So? Does that make me a criminal?"

"No," said Flora.

"Well, all right then."

Ruby stalked upstairs to her room. She shook her bank even though she knew it was empty. She opened her wallet. It held exactly three dollars and ten cents, less than it had held twenty-four hours earlier, since she'd been to the mall in between. She needed money for Christmas presents and she needed it fast. And now with an additional person to shop for — her new cousin — she needed even more money.

If only Ruby were creative like her sister. Flora was going to make a gift for the baby, and that was usually less expensive than buying something. But Ruby had zero interest in sewing or knitting. Or scrapbooking or crafting of any sort. Maybe she could prepare a song to sing to the baby. Last year as a Christmas gift to her family she had performed one of Min's favorite carols. But Ruby didn't think a baby would be interested in Christmas carols. No, she definitely needed a way to earn some money.

Ruby sat on her bed, ignoring the giant ball of clothing and shoes at the foot of it. She remembered something her father had once told her: In order to start a successful business, you have to know your clients, which means knowing your community.

Ruby felt she knew Camden Falls fairly well. She had lived there for less than two years, but because of Needle and Thread, she spent a lot of time on Main Street, and Main Street was the heart of the town. Ruby had walked up and down Main Street countless times. She knew every store and business there, from Needle and Thread to College Pizza, from Dr. Malone's dental practice to the real estate agency. She knew Jackie and Donna, who ran the post office, and Sonny Sutphin, who worked in the second-hand bookstore, and Frank, who owned Frank's Beans, the coffee shop. The family of her new friend Hilary ran the diner and lived above it, and her neighbors the Fongs owned an art gallery. Every now and then a new business came to town (Ruby had seen signs for a magic store that was to open soon), but in general, Ruby felt she knew Main Street. And since she was a member of the Children's Chorus and also took dance lessons, she was acquainted with all sorts of other people, too. Not to mention that she knew every single one of her neighbors in the Row Houses.

Ruby thought and thought, but she didn't know what kind of business to start. Wasn't she a little young to start a business anyway? And didn't starting a business take a lot of time? Ruby needed fast cash. How did kids her age earn money? Baby-sitting? She knew of only one baby — Grace Fong — and Flora always got to sit for her. (Ruby fervently hoped that eventually Aunt Allie would let *Ruby* sit for her cousin.)

Well. This was getting frustrating. It was just one of the many problems associated with being ten years old as opposed to, say, twelve.

Ruby heaved a sigh. Maybe she could pet-sit. But no, in order to get jobs, she would have to wait for the pet owners to go away on trips, and she didn't have time for that.

What else did Ruby know about her community? What did people need? What would they pay other people to do?

What would *I* pay someone to do? Ruby asked herself.

And in an instant, she had her answer. She would pay someone to do all those things that needed doing but that she didn't want to do — cleaning up her room, for instance, or vacuuming the bedrooms (her current household chore).

"That's it!" exclaimed Ruby, jumping to her feet. "I'll be the Doer of Unpleasant Jobs!" Now, that was a business she could actually start. She wouldn't need anything except herself — no store, no equipment. There must be, she thought, any number of unpleasant jobs that people would pay her to do.

Ruby tore down the hall, grabbed the cordless phone from Min's bedside table, and brought it back to her room. She closed her door and dialed Lacey Morris's number. "Lacey!" she cried. "Guess what! I had a brilliant idea. I'm going to start a business. I'm going to be the Doer of Unpleasant Jobs. Do you want to be my partner?"

Lacey Morris, who lived at the left end of the Row Houses with her parents and her sister and brothers, said cautiously, "Your business partner? What would I have to do?"

"Help me with the unpleasant jobs."

"But what kind of unpleasant jobs are we talking about?"

"I don't know. Anything no one wants to do. Cleaning and stuff. All those jobs people keep putting off."

On the other end of the line, Lacey scrunched up

her nose. "There's a reason people keep putting them off."

"Yes," said Ruby. "They're unpleasant."

"Exactly. Which is why I don't think I want to do them." Lacey paused. "I, um, sort of have a lot of allowance money saved up. Besides, I want to put in more practice time on my solo." Lacey also had a solo (a tiny one) in the Thanksgiving concert.

"Okay-ay," sang Ruby, "but you're missing out on a great opportunity." She hung up the phone and punched in Hilary Nelson's number. "Hilary? Do you want to be a Doer of Unpleasant Jobs?"

"What?" said Hilary.

Ruby had to explain her idea again. "So what do you think?" she asked finally.

Hilary paused for so long that Ruby said, "Hello?"

"I'm here. It's just that, well, I told Mom and Dad I'd give them extra help in the diner. This is going to be one of our busiest seasons, you know."

Ruby also knew that Hilary got paid for helping her parents. "I guess I'll just have to do all the unpleasant jobs myself," she said.

"Good luck with that," replied Hilary.

Ruby lifted a pile of papers, library books, and CD's from her desk chair. She wasn't sure where to put them, so she added them to the chaos at the foot of her bed. Then she sat at her desk, a pad of paper before her, and chewed on the end of a pen.

I could, she thought, do unpleasant jobs for people on Main Street. Main Street was, after all, just a couple of blocks from the Row Houses, within easy walking distance. But would storekeepers and business owners *need* a Doer of Unpleasant Jobs? Ruby wasn't sure. Maybe she should start closer to home, with her neighbors.

Ruby crossed her room and stuck her head out into the hallway. "Min!" she called. "I'm going into business! I'm going to do unpleasant jobs. Can I make flyers to give to our neighbors?"

"Which neighbors?" Min called back.

"In the Row Houses."

"Row Houses only? Okay, go ahead."

Ruby sat at her desk again. She wrote:

Do you have unsightly messes?
Are your closets stuffed with unfinished projects?
Do you hate scrubbing and cleaning?
Then call me, the Doer of Unpleasant Jobs!
I'll do anything for

Here Ruby paused, uncertain how much to charge for her work. She would have to discuss that with Min. She turned back to the flyer and added:

Never put off until tomorrow
what you can pay someone else to do today!

Then she hastily drew a star in each corner of the page, sensing that Flora would spend much more time decorating the flyer if it were up to her, which it wasn't.

She grabbed the flyer and rushed across the hall to her sister's room. "Surprise!" she said.

"What?" mumbled Flora, who was lying on her bed, reading *To Kill a Mockingbird*.

"I'm in business." Ruby thrust the flyer at Flora.

"Hey, this is a really good idea," said her sister after she'd read it. "Very practical. And, um, entrepreneurial. Are you sure you don't want to embellish the ad a little more, though? You know, draw —"

"No!" screeched Ruby. "I'm done. Except for the money part. I have to talk to Min about that."

An hour later, her fee decided on and seven flyers (complete with a single star in each corner) printed out on Min's computer, Ruby headed down her walk, ready to get her business rolling. She decided to start with the Morrises and walked briskly in their direction.

The Row Houses, an imposing granite structure built in the 1800s and consisting of eight attached and nearly identical homes, had once belonged to wealthy Camden Falls families, families who could afford maids and butlers and gardeners. The current families, to Ruby's relief, did not employ maids or butlers or gardeners, which was exactly why they might need Ruby.

Ruby rang the Morrises' bell, and could hear Lacey practicing her solo inside. I really ought to be practicing my own solos, she thought. (She had two — a tiny one like Lacey's and a much longer one.) While she was at it, it couldn't hurt to start practicing her even bigger solo for the Christmas concert.

Oh, well, thought Ruby. I have time.

The sound of the bell brought thundering feet to the door, which was flung open by Alyssa, the youngest Morris, proudly exclaiming, "I got here first!"

"Can you give this to your mom and dad?" Ruby asked, handing her one of the flyers. "It's very important. I've gone into business."

Alyssa took the flyer, silenced by the grandeur of Ruby's announcement.

Ruby headed next door to the house that until recently had belonged to the Willets but now belonged to the Hamiltons. She hesitated before ringing the bell and then reminded herself that strange Mrs. Hamilton wasn't there; Ruby would not have to face her. Was it okay to feel relieved that Mrs. Hamilton was in the hospital — a *mental* hospital? Probably not, but Ruby felt relieved anyway. And when Willow Hamilton, who was Flora's new friend, opened the door, Ruby gave her a genuine smile. "Anything that needs doing, I can do it!" she proclaimed.

Ruby continued down the row. She handed a flyer to Margaret Malone, Dr. Malone's older daughter, skipped her own house, and rang the bell of Olivia

Walter. Olivia answered the door and took the flyer with interest. "Maybe I could pay you to do something about my brothers," she said.

Mr. Pennington, who lived next to Olivia, wasn't home, although Ruby could hear old Jacques barking on the other side of the door. She left a flyer under a rock on the front stoop and knocked at the Edwardses'.

"Ruby! Ruby! Good morning!" Robby Edwards exclaimed enthusiastically when he answered the door. "Look, I'm still in my pajamas! I don't have to work at Sincerely Yours today, that's why," he added, as if Ruby had asked.

Robby, who was eighteen and had Down syndrome (and who was one of Ruby's favorite people), worked at the store recently opened by Olivia Walter's parents. Ruby handed him a flyer.

"What's this?" asked Robby, squinting at it. "The Doer of Unpleasant Jobs? That's you?"

"Yup," said Ruby proudly. "I can do anything at all." She leaned forward and whispered, "I need money."

"Oh," said Robby knowingly.

"So be sure to give that to your mom and dad."

"Right-o," Robby replied, and closed the door.

Ruby visited the last house in the row, the Fongs', but no one answered the bell, so she slipped the flyer under a corner of their doormat.

Now all she had to do was sit back and wait for the phone to ring. Ruby would be rich in no time.

CHAPTER 3

Sunday Afternoon, November 22nd

The car that was spinning its way from Camden Falls, Massachusetts, to New York City contained two suitcases, a car seat for an infant, and one person, the driver, Allie Read. Allie drove steadily. The car was silent. No music was playing and the radio was turned off. Allie needed to think, and she was glad for the quiet of the car — no distractions. No phone calls, no doorbells, no e-mail.

Allie wanted to be in New York already and wished she could will herself there, but she was also grateful for this small island of time in which to mull over the great change that was suddenly taking place in her life.

A baby on the way.

How long had Allie wished for this?

Years. She had wished for it for years. She had wished for it when she was a girl and wanted to be the mommy instead of the little sister, and she had wished for it when she and Paul had dreamed of their wedding and their life together afterward, and she had wished and wished for it, harder than ever, after Paul had left her.

A baby on the way.

That morning, Allie had tossed the two suitcases into the backseat of her car. One was full of her things — enough clothes for a week in Manhattan — and one was full of things for a baby — mostly for a baby girl, since she had once been so sure that she and Paul would adopt a girl from China. But the adoption process, Allie had learned quickly, could be long and complicated and unpredictable. She might still adopt a baby from China or some other country. Someday. But right now a baby in New York needed her.

The highway hummed along, spreading out before and behind Allie's car, and she thought of the trip she had made to Camden Falls almost a year earlier. It had been her first trip back home in a very long time, and she had made it because Paul was suddenly gone. He had left her the way people leave in movies. She had woken up one morning to find his side of the bed empty. (This was not unusual since he liked to be at his office by eight o'clock, and Allie worked at home as a writer.) But that morning a note was pinned to his pillow. Actually *pinned* to it. Allie had imagined him rummaging through their drawers, searching for an elusive safety pin. The note had said simply: *Allie, I won't be coming back. I've known for a long time that things aren't right between us. Sorry. Paul.*

What on earth did that mean? *Allie* hadn't known things weren't right between them. Didn't something like that deserve a discussion? A phone call at the very least? But there had been no discussion or phone call, only an e-mail later in the day saying that he would come by on Saturday to pack up his things, and that if Allie didn't want to see him, she should arrange to be out of the apartment.

That particular Saturday was the Saturday after Thanksgiving. Not long after Paul had collected his things (Allie decided not to speak to him and fled to Debbie and David's apartment for the day), Allie had written to Min saying she wanted to come home for Christmas. To everyone's surprise, including Allie's, she hadn't returned to New York for months. Christmas came and went, New Year's Eve came and went, and Allie found that she had no interest in living in the old apartment in the city. Eventually, she sold the apartment, bought a house in Camden Falls, and the town in which she had grown up became her home again. And now it would be the town in which she would raise her own child.

A baby on the way.

Allie looked at her watch, looked at the speedometer, checked the gas gauge. Her thoughts turned to her conversation with Mrs. Prescott the previous evening.

When Allie had recovered from her shock ("The birth parents chose me to adopt their baby?!"), she asked Mrs. Prescott question after question. Dozens of questions.

Which was why Allie was now reasonably sure that the baby would not in fact be born during the week that she could stay in New York, and that she would be returning to Camden Falls empty-handed. The baby would almost certainly come home later. And yet, Allie had packed a suitcase full of baby things, of lacy pink and yellow dresses and bonnets.

Allie smiled. "I hope the baby is a girl," she said aloud. "Otherwise, I'll have to buy an entire new wardrobe." Which, of course, she would happily do. Boy or girl, Allie didn't care. She just wanted to be a mom.

Allie drove past a green sign reading NEW YORK CITY — 24 MILES. She drew in a breath, felt her pulse quicken. She was excited, but she was also frightened, she realized. What if the baby was born prematurely and there were complications? That could happen. That was why the doctors wanted to delay the birth. What if the birth parents decided to keep their baby? What if Allie brought the baby home to Camden Falls and found out that raising a child on her own was harder than she had thought it was going to be? She knew she would have lots of help, starting with Min and Flora and Ruby, but still . . .

Half an hour later, her heart now pounding, Allie crossed into Manhattan. She headed for the West Side Highway and drove past the familiar sights — the Hudson River, with its boats and barges, and Riverside Park, where she and Paul occasionally took Sunday morning walks (even though the park was far from their neighborhood in the West Village) and watched the children in the playgrounds and the dogs in the dog runs.

At 30th Street Allie turned east, drove to 7th Avenue, threaded her way south to 14th Street, and finally found a parking space just half a block from her friends' apartment on 12th Street. Her old neighborhood. Allie unloaded her suitcases, locked the car, and fervently hoped she wouldn't see Paul somewhere, his arm slung casually across another woman's shoulders, their heads bent in discussion.

She lugged the suitcases to the entrance of David and Debbie's apartment building and was cheered to see that Shef was on duty at the front desk.

"Good afternoon!" he greeted her. "I haven't seen you in a long time."

"Hi, Shef." Allie smiled. "It's nice to see you. Did Debbie and David tell you I'll be using their apartment this week?"

In answer, Shef pulled a set of keys out of the desk drawer and held them aloft. "Everything's ready for you. Let me know if you have any problems. Do you want a cart for your luggage?" He handed her the keys.

Ten minutes later, Allie walked breathlessly through the door of the apartment that she hadn't seen in a year. She wanted to walk through it slowly, to look at the view from each window, but instead she pulled her cell phone from her purse and checked it for messages. Not a single one. Even so, she called Mrs. Prescott. "Any word?" she asked, knowing what the answer would be.

"Sorry," Mrs. Prescott replied. "Nothing yet. But that's good news. The mother is resting and the baby is staying where he — or she — belongs."

Allie closed her cell phone and settled in to wait.

CHAPTER 4

Monday, November 23rd

If you were to look at a postcard of Camden Falls, Massachusetts, you might see a small town nestled in the hills, or you might see Main Street, with its rows of shops and businesses, or you might see gracious old homes, some dating all the way back to colonial times. But if those photos were taken in the summer, as were many of the ones that grace the postcards sold in the T-shirt Emporium or Stuff 'n' Nonsense or the bookstores, you would not have a picture of Camden Falls at the beginning of the holiday season.

For *this* is Camden Falls on the Monday before Thanksgiving: A feeling of expectation is in the air, a feeling of festivity, too. Hanging in shopwindows are wreaths of autumn flowers and bunches of dried corn. The trees lining Main Street are bare. Soon, they'll be twined with tiny gold lights, but not until next weekend. The residents of Camden Falls don't start decorating for Christmas until Thanksgiving is over.

At the edges of the sidewalks and on the roofs of the stores are traces of the season's first snow. It fell last night, just a flurry, really, but it sent Ruby Northrop and Lacey Morris and plenty of other Camden Falls children into a fit of excitement about future snow days and the possibility of blizzards.

Take a walk along Main Street and look at it up close. Here is the Marquis Diner, ready for its first Thanksgiving in Camden Falls. It's owned by the Nelsons, and they've hung a banner in the window announcing that it will be open for business on Thanksgiving Day, serving traditional turkey dinners in addition to everything they usually serve. Here is Fig Tree, the fanciest restaurant in town, the menu in the display case outside the front door bordered with pumpkins and cornucopias. Here is Needle and Thread, the sewing store owned by Min, and by Olivia Walter's grandmother Gigi. Christmas fabrics and trimmings have been for sale since the summer, but the store window still features back-to-school clothing and two quilted Thanksgiving table runners (made by Gigi). No matter what, Min and Gigi will not break with town tradition and decorate their window for Christmas before Thanksgiving has come and gone. Three doors down from Needle and Thread is Sincerely Yours, the store recently opened by Olivia's parents. In its windows are gift baskets filled with artificial chrysanthemums and chocolate turkeys and candles shaped like corncobs.

Now cross the street and walk to the south end of town, past the movie theatre. Here is something exciting. A new business has opened today. The sign out front reads MATY'S MAGIC STORE, and this afternoon it's drawing a crowd.

"Look at that!" says Ruby breathlessly. She has walked to Main Street after school with Lacey and Hilary, and they're gawking at the outside of Maty's.

"A magician's hat," says Lacey. "How did they do that?"

The front of the store has been transformed into an enormous top hat, out of which sticks a pair of pink-and-white rabbit ears.

Hilary reads a sign posted in the front window. "'Magic galore,'" she says. "'Tricks, illusions' . . . hmm. A 'Who-Done-It Party.' I wonder what that is."

"This is so cool," says Ruby. "I'm going to do my Christmas shopping here."

"In a magic store?" asks Hilary dubiously.

"Yes," replies Ruby. "If I ever earn any money. It's really a shame that Aunt Allie didn't win the lottery. Oh, well. Come on. Let's go inside."

If you want a complete picture of Camden Falls, you'll have to leave Main Street behind now. It may be the heart of town, but you'll want to see what lies beyond. Walk west until you reach a tiny cottage plunked down amid gardens, so many gardens that there's no actual yard. The gardens trail from the sidewalk to the house and don't stop there, since ivy climbs the walls. This is the home of Mary Woolsey, who, thinks Flora Northrop, could be a character in a picture book. She's a little old lady like Miss Rumphius or the one with the shoe and all the children. Except that she doesn't have any children. She has two ancient cats, though, who in cat years are probably older than Mary. Mary, who works part-time at Needle and Thread, has lived alone for a long time and is happy in her solitude, although she's also happy that Flora has become her friend. Mary will be celebrating Thanksgiving by herself, and she doesn't mind that at all.

If you feel like taking a long walk on this fine but chilly day, you could hike out the county road, past the turnoffs for Minnewaska State Park and Davidson's Orchards, until you came to a house all by itself in the country. At this hour of the afternoon, the house is empty. It's the home of Nikki Sherman, whose best friends are Olivia, Flora, and Ruby. Until Flora and Ruby moved to town, Nikki had no close friends at all. And now she has three. Nikki's life has not been easy, but in the last year it has changed so much that she sometimes thinks about her younger self as an entirely different person. Her alcoholic father is gone — Nikki isn't sure where, and she doesn't care as long as he never bothers her family again. Her mother now holds down a job that a year ago she could only have dreamed about. Nikki's older brother, who once drifted along, unsure what he wanted to do with his life, is a freshman in college (to everyone's surprise), and Nikki can't wait until he comes home for the Thanksgiving break. This afternoon, Nikki is on her way back from Camden Falls Central High School. The bus will shortly deposit her at the end of the gravel lane leading to her house, where she'll be greeted with boisterous barking by Paw-Paw, and later with hugs by her mother and her little sister, Mae, who's at her after-school program. Nikki misses having her family around during these hours, but she relishes the peace she finds at home, something that was foreign to her for most of her life.

Several miles from Nikki's house, also on the outskirts of Camden Falls, is Three Oaks, the continuing-care retirement community, and this is where Mrs. Sherman found her dream job. The job, which might not, Nikki knows, be a dream job for some people, consists of managing the dining room at Three Oaks. This is demanding and requires Mrs. Sherman to work long hours and often to be at Three Oaks on weekends and holidays. But the pay is good and Mrs. Sherman is grateful to have been selected to fill the position.

Three Oaks is where the Willets live now, and as Mr. Willet leaves his apartment this afternoon and walks through the complex to the wing where his wife, Mary Lou, resides, he notes with pleasure that his new home has put on its holiday face, just as Main Street has. Mr. Willet walks past the Three Oaks barbershop, the Three Oaks gift shop, the Three Oaks coffee shop, and the Three Oaks craft room (all located in the main building) and sees autumn flower arrangements and gourds and even a few carved pumpkins left over from Halloween. He passes into the hospital wing and smiles at the cardboard Pilgrims and cheery HAPPY THANKSGIVING! banner that decorate the nurses' station. As he enters Mary Lou's room, he reminds himself that his wife may or may not remember who he is — this will depend on whether she's having a good day or a bad day — and decides that if she doesn't remember him, he can try to cheer himself with thoughts about Thanksgiving, and the guests he's invited to join him and Mary Lou in the dining room on Thursday.

Leave Three Oaks behind now and return to Camden Falls. If you walk along Aiken Avenue, you'll pass the Row Houses (there's Mr. Pennington snapping a leash to Jacques's collar), and after a few blocks you'll reach the road that leads to Aunt Allie's house. On this afternoon, the door of her home is shut tight and no lights shine inside. The house, like Allie, is waiting.

CHAPTER 5

Tuesday Afternoon,
November 24ᵗʰ

Aunt Allie might not have won the lottery, but Ruby Northrop thought that she could feel her own luck changing. For one thing, there was the new baby. A baby on the way who would be her cousin and who would live right in her town. Ruby had never had a cousin nearby and was slightly jealous of Olivia, who had many cousins living near Camden Falls. Then there was the fact that Ruby had gotten a 98 on a spelling test for which she had forgotten to study. Ruby was not noted for her good grades, so this unexpected 98 — surely an A — went right along with all the good things that had been happening lately.

Given her run of luck, she wasn't very surprised to come home from school on Monday, having paid her visit to Maty's Magic Store, to find two exciting messages for her on the answering machine.

"Ruby!" Flora had called from the kitchen. "Come here!"

Ruby was still shrugging out of her backpack. She hustled into the kitchen, shedding clothing and school supplies as she went, a trail of sneakers, papers, a sweater, her social studies book, and finally the backpack itself, now empty.

"What? What?" she cried.

"You got two replies to your ad!" said Flora. "Listen!" She pressed the REPLAY button on the machine.

"Hi, Ruby."

"That's Dr. Malone!" exclaimed Ruby.

"*Shh!* Listen," said Flora.

"Margaret showed me your flyer, and there are a couple of chores here we'd love to hand over to you," continued Dr. Malone. "There's some stuff in the basement that needs to be cleaned out. . . . Well, I'll give you the details when you call back. You can reach me at the office before six or at home tonight. I'll talk to you later. Bye."

"And now," said Flora, waving her hand over the answering machine like a magician, "call number two."

"Hello, Ruby? Ruby? This is Robby. Is this your answering machine? Ruby? Okay. Mom told me to call you. We have a job for you."

"Yes! Yes!" squealed Ruby.

"It's unpleasant," Robby added.

"That's my specialty," Ruby told Flora with what she hoped was a professional edge to her voice. "Unpleasant jobs."

"So call back," Robby finished up.

"Wow, Ruby, that's great," said Flora. "Two jobs and you only handed out the flyers yesterday. I guess you're in business."

Ruby wasted no time returning Dr. Malone's and Robby's calls. When she had hung up, she plunked herself at the kitchen table with Flora and reported, "Dr. Malone wants me to clean out part of his basement, like he said, and also I'm supposed to alphabetize Margaret's CD's." She paused thoughtfully. "Huh. I don't think I'd want my CD's in alphabetical order. I kind of like them messy. But Margaret isn't a messy sort of person."

"No, she isn't," Flora agreed.

"Then I talked to Robby's mother," Ruby went on, "and she said they have this huge pile of old clothes they want to donate to the clothing bank, but they're all in a heap, and they need to be sorted by season and then folded neatly and put into bags. She said they've been putting this off for years. Years — can you imagine?" Ruby bit into a chocolate chip cookie. "I bet I can do it in one hour. Tops."

"But don't rush your work," said Flora maddeningly. "You have to do a good job."

"I know, I know."

"Or people won't call you back with *more* jobs."

"I *know*."

"Okay."

Ruby thought that if she ran directly to the

Edwardses' after school the next day, took care of the clothes, and then hurried to the Malones' (arriving just as Margaret returned from high school), she could handle both jobs in one afternoon. She also thought that she should have a uniform, so that night she found an old white T-shirt and, with a fat black permanent marker, wrote DOER OF UNPLEASANT JOBS across the back and, in smaller letters on the front, RUBY.

She wore the T-shirt under her sweater at school the next day, so that when she arrived at Robby's house, all she had to do was remove her sweater and she was ready to work.

"The clothes are in here," said Mrs. Edwards, guiding Ruby upstairs to a spare room. "We certainly are happy to let you take care of this for us."

Ruby stopped at the threshold of the room and stared. She thought that, outside of a department store, she had never seen so many clothes all in one place.

Mrs. Edwards looked apologetic. "As I said, we've been putting this chore off for a while."

Ruby held up a small striped shirt. "Whose is this?" she asked.

"Well, it *was* Robby's. When he was in first grade. That's about how long the clothes have been piling up."

Ruby swallowed hard but didn't say anything.

"So what you need to do," said Mrs. Edwards, "is decide whether the clothes are for summer or winter, fold them, and pack them into bags." She indicated a stack of paper grocery bags by the door. "Leave the summer clothes up here, and I'll help you carry the bags of winter clothes downstairs. I'm going to drive them to the clothing bank tomorrow. The director said they're only interested in the cold-weather clothes at the moment."

"Okay," replied Ruby, who was already wondering whether she would be able to arrive at the Malones' on time.

Mrs. Edwards left and Ruby dove into the job. She sorted first, making decisions fast. When she had two piles (enormous, teetering piles) of clothes — one for summer and one for winter — she began to fold them. Folding was not one of Ruby's strong points (as she had once heard Min mention to Flora), but she concentrated and did her best. It occurred to her that she *could* simply stuff most of the clothes into the bags and fold only the ones on the top — that would make the job go much more quickly — but Flora's words about being called back for future jobs rang in her ears, so she worked doggedly, folding each article carefully. And when she had finished, she was surprised to look at her watch and see that in fact just over an hour had passed. Not bad at all. She would arrive at Margaret's only fifteen minutes late.

"Ruby," said Mrs. Edwards as they lugged the last bag of winter clothes to the front door, "I will certainly call you in the future. You did a great job. I can't tell you how much I appreciate this." And she pressed several bills into Ruby's hand.

Ruby, glowing, sprinted to the Malones' house. "What do you want me to do first?" she asked, the moment Margaret opened the door.

"Hi, Ruby," said Margaret. "Nice to see you. Thank you for coming."

"Oh. Yeah. Sorry to be in a rush, but I'm trying to stay on schedule," Ruby replied, shedding her coat and sweater.

Margaret smiled at the sight of Ruby's shirt. "Very nice lettering," she said.

"Thanks. It's my uniform." Ruby clapped her hands together smartly. "Okay. Basement or CD's?" she asked.

"Up to you. Why don't I take you down to the basement and show you the stuff Dad wants cleaned up. Then you can decide where to begin."

Ruby followed Margaret into the Malones' kitchen, and Margaret opened the door to the basement. Ruby's nose was greeted with the familiar basementy smell that all the cellars in the Row Houses seemed to share. A smell of dampness and cement and something that Min described as "fustiness." Ruby wasn't sure what "fustiness" meant, but it sounded like a good description of a basement smell.

Margaret switched on the light, and she and Ruby made their way down the worn wooden steps.

"It's over here," said Margaret, indicating an area of the basement beyond the Malones' washer and dryer.

Ruby stopped and stared. "*That?*" she cried.

Margaret cleared her throat. "I know it's a lot. I mean, it looks like a lot. But it isn't, really, and all you need to do is toss out the stuff that's completely useless and organize the rest of it."

"But," said Ruby, gawking at what appeared to be a miniature mountain of junk, "how do I know what's useless to *you*?" She remembered that her mother used to say: "One man's trash is another man's treasure."

"Oh, you'll know," said Margaret. She grabbed at something, and Ruby now saw that the mountain was actually overflowing storage shelves. "This, for example," Margaret continued, pulling a scarred pole from the top of the heap on a middle shelf.

"What is it?" asked Ruby.

Margaret shrugged. "Exactly. A mop without the mop part? A broom without the broom part? I don't know. And if you don't know, either, then there isn't any point in keeping it."

Ruby nodded. "I understand."

"So do you want to start here or in my room?"

"I might as well start here," replied Ruby weakly, the dark recesses of the cellar already reminding her of the many reasons she avoided descending into Min's basement.

"Okay. Just leave the stuff to be thrown out over there by the washer and then tidy up the shelves. If you have any questions, call me. I'll be right upstairs in the kitchen."

Margaret climbed the steps, and Ruby stood before the shelves. Tentatively, she reached for a lumpy item. Her fingers had barely closed over it when she heard a noise from a distant corner, a sort of scratchy, slithery noise. Please don't be a ghost, she thought fervently. Or a snake. She reminded herself that ghosts weren't real (probably) and that snakes weren't around in late November (probably), and hefted the item, which turned out to be a boot. She set it aside. If she found its mate, she would return the pair to the shelves. If she didn't, the lone boot would be destined for the dump.

Ruby worked steadily, ignoring creepy basement sounds, and found that the job went fairly quickly. "Margaret!" she called forty-five minutes later. "I think I'm done." She surveyed her work with satisfaction. The shelves, emptied of nearly half their contents, now neatly held the remaining tools, baskets, outdoor clothing, and other articles Ruby had deemed worth keeping. And in a pile by the washing machine were heaped a bucket with a hole in its side, two cans of dried-up paint, the single boot, the broom handle, and many broken items, some of which Ruby couldn't identify.

"Wow!" exclaimed Margaret, before she was even

halfway down the stairs. "Ruby, this is fantastic. Dad's going to be thrilled. I've never seen the basement look so good."

"Thank you," said Ruby modestly.

"Do you still have time for my CD's?"

Ruby looked at her watch. It was closer to dinner than she had thought it would be, her jobs so far having gone fairly quickly but still having been bigger than Ruby had imagined, and she didn't want to upset Min. She also didn't want to turn down perfectly good work, so she phoned Flora and told her she'd be home in an hour (she hoped).

And then she climbed up the stairs to Margaret's room.

She saw a mound of CD's on the bed. A mound, not a mountain. Not nearly as many CD's as Ruby had feared she might find.

She let out her breath. "Okay," she said. "How should I alphabetize them? By title?"

Margaret, who was standing in the doorway, shook her head. "By the artist's name."

"Artist . . ." repeated Ruby.

"The performer," Margaret explained.

Ruby set to work.

An hour later, she opened the door to her house. She was as tired as she had ever been, but her pocket was stuffed with bills and she was quite pleased with her first day as the Doer of Unpleasant Jobs.

"Ruby!" Min called from the kitchen. "You have just enough time to eat a quick dinner before your rehearsal."

Rehearsal. Ruby had completely forgotten that she had a chorus rehearsal that evening — the final rehearsal before the Thanksgiving concert.

"Um," said Ruby as she entered the kitchen. "Um, I don't really need to go to the rehearsal."

"Don't need to go? What about your solos?" asked Min.

Ruby blew hair from her face. She was grimy. She was starving. And all she wanted to do was fall into her bed.

"I know my solos," said Ruby. She opened the refrigerator. "Only one is really important anyway, and I know it like the back of my hand." She peered around the door of the fridge and met Min's eyes.

"Are you certain?" asked Min.

Before Ruby could answer, the phone rang and Min lunged for it. "That's Allie, I think," she said.

Ruby knew that the subject of rehearsal was over. She told herself she could practice her solos by herself anytime she felt like it. She had an entire day and a half before the concert.

CHAPTER 6

Wednesday Afternoon, November 25ᵗʰ

"Nikki?" said Mae Sherman. "On the first Thanksgiving, didn't the Pilgrims freeze?"

"What?" replied Nikki. She took her sister's hand and together they walked along the lane to their house. It was one-thirty on the day before Thanksgiving. School had let out early, and Nikki had been given only minimal homework. The holiday weekend stretched ahead of her deliciously.

"Didn't the Pilgrims freeze on the first Thanksgiving?" Mae repeated.

"I don't understand," said Nikki. "What do you mean?"

"Well, all the pictures show them having Thanksgiving dinner at a big picnic table outside, in the woods or someplace. But Miss Drew said the Pilgrims lived here in New England, like we do. And it's freezing here by Thanksgiving time." Mae held out her mittened hands to indicate just how cold it was.

"Maybe —" Nikki started to say.

"*And*," Mae barged on, "in the pictures, the Pilgrims are always just wearing their regular Pilgrim clothes. They aren't wearing coats or mittens, and anyway, how could they cut their turkey if they were wearing mittens? So what I'm asking is, weren't they freezing?"

Nikki considered Mae's questions as they approached their house. She wished mightily that Mae had gone to her after-school program as usual, but there was no program on the Wednesday before Thanksgiving, so Nikki was stuck with the Pilgrim problem. "I think," she said, "that the first Thanksgiving was celebrated earlier in the fall, when it was warmer. But maybe you should ask Miss Drew about that on Monday," she added delicately.

"That means you don't really know the answer!" Mae sounded gleeful.

"True. I don't know the answer. I don't know lots of answers. Do you know all the answers?"

"No, but I'm only seven," replied Mae. "You're twelve."

"Well, I guess that just goes to show that twelve-year-olds don't know all the answers, either."

"Maybe eighteen-year-olds do," said Mae. "I'll ask Tobias when he gets home."

"Oh, don't bother him with that. Let him relax a —"

"*Bother* him!" cried Mae indignantly. "That is not a bothery question. It's a perfectly good one."

Nikki sensed tears and hastily changed the subject. "Remember what we're going to do this afternoon," she said. "First thing. Well, first thing after we let Paw-Paw out."

Mae brightened. "The baskets! We get to fill the baskets! But shouldn't we wait for Tobias? Won't he want to help us?"

"Do you want to wait for him? He might not be home for another hour."

"I want to wait," said Mae firmly. "He shouldn't miss out on the fun."

"Actually, he doesn't even know about our secret project yet."

Several weeks earlier, Nikki and Mae and their mother had begun to plan a Thanksgiving surprise. It had started when Nikki had said, "Remember all those years when we found baskets of food on our doorstep at Thanksgiving? We got turkeys and everything."

"Who left the baskets?" Mae had asked.

"Well, charity," Mrs. Sherman had replied.

"Who's Charity?"

"Not who, what," Nikki had said, and then she and her mother had tried to explain "charity" to Mae.

Finally, Mrs. Sherman had said, "But this year we don't need any charity."

"You know what?" Nikki had exclaimed. "I just had a great idea! This year *we* could give baskets away. I mean, not with turkeys. I know we couldn't afford to do that. But we could put together baskets of cookies and stuff."

"Who would we give them to?" Mae had asked.

"To people who need them. People who are lonely, like Mary Woolsey."

"Or to people who have been nice to us in the past," Mrs. Sherman had said. "Like Mrs. DuVane. She may be a little forward, but she's been very generous to our family for a long time."

And so it had been decided that on the day before Thanksgiving, Nikki and Mae and Tobias would secretly deliver baskets of goodies to several people in Camden Falls.

"I can't wait! I can't wait! I can't wait!" chanted Mae now as Nikki unlocked the door to the house. Paw-Paw rushed outside the moment the door was open, nearly knocking Mae over in the process.

"Wow. He must really need to poo," Mae remarked.

Nikki decided to let the comment go. "Come on. Put your school things away. Let's at least get the baskets ready to be filled. We can make an assembly line while we wait for Tobias."

"What's an assembly line?"

"Like in a factory. I'll show you."

Nikki cleared the kitchen table. "We'll put all the baskets on this end," she said, "and then piles of the things that will go in the baskets. We'll stack the dish towels here and the bags of cookies here, and then make a pile of the candy boxes here, and put the Pilgrim candles over here" (Nikki sincerely hoped that the mention of Pilgrims wouldn't rekindle the question of the first Thanksgiving's weather) "and the dried flowers here, and all the autumn leaves you found here. See? And then we'll take something from each pile and put it in the basket."

The assembly line had just been organized when the front door burst open and in walked Tobias.

"You're here!" squawked Mae.

"You're here early!" cried Nikki.

"Happy Thanksgiving!" said Tobias, dropping a bulging bag of laundry on the floor.

He hugged his sisters, and before he had even let them go, Mae was exclaiming, "You have to see our project! You can help us with it. We've been planning it forever, and today we get to give the baskets out. It's a secret. It's going to be so much fun!"

"What?" said Tobias.

Nikki explained the project to him in a more orderly fashion, and presently, she and Mae and Tobias began filling the baskets. They lined each one with an autumn dish towel, filled it with the treats, decorated it with the flowers and leaves, and tied an anonymous Happy Thanksgiving card to the handle.

There were six baskets in all.

"So who are they for?" asked Tobias as they worked.

"One is for Mrs. DuVane," said Nikki. "That was Mom's idea. Because of everything she's done for us. And one is for Mary Woolsey."

"That's nice," commented Tobias.

"One is for Miss Drew," said Mae blissfully.

"Her teacher," Nikki informed Tobias.

"He knows that," Mae said and then added, "I love Miss Drew."

"One is for a woman named Mrs. Bradley. You don't know her, but I met her last year when Mr. Pennington took Flora and Olivia and Ruby and me on his Special Delivery route. We were handing out Christmas baskets, and Mrs. Bradley . . ." Nikki paused, thinking. "Well, it just seemed like there was no one else in her life at all. She needs a walker to get around and I don't think she ever leaves her house. She was so grateful for our visit that she almost cried, and she told us we were her Christmas angels and gave us chocolates."

"Chocolates?" said Mae with interest.

"Do you remember where she lives?" asked Tobias.

"Yup," said Nikki. "All right. Let me see." She counted on her fingers. "Okay, that's four baskets. The fifth one is for Willow Hamilton and her family. They *really* need cheering up. Mrs. Hamilton probably won't be out of the hospital until February. Plus, they've only lived here for a few weeks and they don't know many people."

"Paulie's family really needs cheering up, too," said Mae. "The last basket is for them."

"Who's Paulie?" asked Tobias.

"He's in my grade but in Mr. Hawthorne's class. He has . . . what's it called, Nikki?"

"Leukemia," she replied.

"And his hair fell out and he's always absent. He only went to four days of second grade and then he got sick. I mostly remember him from first grade."

"He's an only child," added Nikki, glancing at her brother.

"Wow," said Tobias softly.

"I know."

"Well, it sounds like you guys chose people who will really like the baskets. All right. Let me think about how to get to their houses. Do you know where Paulie lives, Mae?"

She nodded. "Near school."

"What if these people are at home?" asked Tobias. "You want to deliver the baskets in secret, don't you?"

"Like elves," replied Mae.

"If anyone's at home . . ." Nikki started to say. "Well, hmm. I don't know. We'll play that by ear."

"Okay," said Tobias. "Everyone grab two baskets and let's get going."

They started with Mrs. Bradley.

"This one will be easy," said Nikki as they parked outside of her house. "Not to be callous, but seriously, it will take her so long to answer the door that we could ring her bell, run back to the car, and be gone before she's even on her feet. We have to ring the bell," she added, "because otherwise she might never find the basket."

"I'll sit here with the engine running," said Tobias. "You guys run as fast as you can — and just hope she doesn't see you out the window."

Laughing, Nikki and Mae rushed to Mrs. Bradley's door. Nikki rang the bell and then whispered, "Run!" She and Mae sped back to the car and Tobias drove away.

"I wanted to watch her find the basket!" cried Mae.

"Nope. Too risky," said Nikki. "That might spoil the surprise."

"Elves wouldn't stick around to watch," added Tobias.

Mrs. DuVane's house was next. It was large, lights were on inside, and three cars were parked in the cir- cular drive in front. Tobias came to a slow stop on the road. "What do you think?" he asked Nikki.

"We could come back," she said.

"No. We'd better leave the basket now."

"I could tiptoe up to her front door with it," said Mae, "and just leave it. I'll be as quiet as a mouse."

In the end, that was what they decided to do. And it

worked. Mae flew triumphantly back to the car, minus the basket, and said, "Floor it!" to Tobias, who left in a hurry but did not floor it. "I don't think anyone saw me," Mae added.

The next two houses — Willow Hamilton's and Mary's — were easy because Nikki knew no one would be at home. The baskets were left on the front door-steps to be discovered later in the afternoon.

"Miss Drew is next!" exclaimed Mae as Tobias pulled away from Mary's house. "Oh, she is going to be *so* surprised. For days and days she'll wonder who mysteriously left a Thanksgiving basket at her door."

"Are you sure you're going to be able to keep the secret?" asked Nikki suspiciously.

Mae nodded solemnly. "Elves don't tell."

Tobias drove across Camden Falls to the small house that Mae swore belonged to her teacher.

"Looks like no one is home here, either," said Nikki. "There's no car in the driveway."

"Well, just in case," said Tobias, "Mae, you duck down and hide, and Nikki, you run the basket to the door. That way even if Miss Drew sees you, she won't know who you are."

"But she does know me," said Nikki. "You go, Tobias."

"Me? No way! I have to drive the getaway car."

In the end it was decided that Nikki should take the basket after all, and she hustled it to the front door, feeling the same anticipation and excitement she'd felt when she ran to Mrs. Bradley's house. Being the keeper of a secret, the bearer of a gift, sparked a warmth in her, a rare kind of joy that she had experienced only a few times in her life. She returned, grinning, to the car.

"One last basket," said Tobias.

"Paulie's," said Mae. She directed her brother to Paulie's house.

"We might not be able to deliver this one in secret," remarked Tobias as he parked the car. "Look."

Several people were standing on Paulie's front porch, and Paulie and his mother were talking to them at the door.

"Well, we'll come back later," said Nikki.

But Mae said, "No. You know what? This one doesn't have to be a secret." And in a flash, she opened the car door and dashed along the walk to the porch.

"Hi, Paulie," Nikki heard her sister say. "Happy Thanksgiving. This is from me and my family."

Nikki watched Paulie, who was indeed bald and was wearing pajamas and slippers, take the basket from Mae.

"Thanks!" he exclaimed. "Look, Mom."

Paulie's mother turned to Mae. "Who are —" she started to ask.

"Just a Thanksgiving elf!" Mae replied, and ran back to the car. She slid in next to Nikki and said,

"Thanksgiving's not even here and I feel like we already had a holiday."

On the drive home, Mae's head drooped against Nikki's shoulder. Before she fell asleep, she said, "Let's do this again next year."

CHAPTER 7

Wednesday Afternoon, November 25ᵗʰ

There was nothing like New York City during the holidays. Allie was convinced of that. She had lived in New York for many years, and while she had grown tired of it and found that she was now happier in tiny Camden Falls, there were things she missed about the city, and one of them was the way the old town got dressed for the holidays. And Allie felt that it got dressed as surely as an actor put on a costume to play a role on the stage. Decorations — some brand-new and some decades old — were brought out, and slowly New York was transformed from a grimy gray labyrinth into a sparkling magical kingdom. A giant tree appeared in Rockefeller Center near the end of November, and by the beginning of December had been decorated with thousands of tiny lights and was heralded by two rows of twinkly angels. Allie found that if she squinted her eyes and looked at only the grand tree and the skaters on the rink below, she might be a visitor in Old England.

Then, thought Allie, there was the enormous lighted snowflake that would be suspended above Fifth Avenue, and the blazing trees up and down Park Avenue, and another lighted tree at Lincoln Center, and the windows at Tiffany, Saks, and, best of all, Lord & Taylor. Each year she marveled at the way a single plain window could become a scene from a Victorian Christmas or a sleigh ride through the woods or the start of Santa's enchanted flight around the world.

On Wednesday afternoon, while Nikki and Tobias and Mae were delivering their baskets in Camden Falls, Allie was looking out the window of the apartment in Manhattan, drinking in the sights of the city as it put on its holiday garb. She hadn't heard from Mrs. Prescott, and while she knew that this was actually a good thing, since it meant that the baby was staying put and growing bigger and healthier before the birth, she found that she felt, as Min would say, antsy. She couldn't sit still. All she could think about were the baby and the mom and whether they would be okay and whether the parents would want their baby to be adopted after all and how bringing a baby home to Camden Falls would *really* feel. The thoughts tumbled around in Allie's head until she was so antsy that she decided to take a walk. She checked to make sure her cell phone was on, set the ringer to the opening bars of "Jingle Bells," turned the volume up high, and slipped the phone into an inside pocket of her coat. There. No matter where she went that afternoon or what she decided to do, she would hear her cell phone if Mrs. Prescott called with news.

Allie left the apartment on 12th Street, turned east, walked to Fifth Avenue, and then decided to walk all the way to Midtown. She could stay on Fifth Avenue, she told herself, or she could make detours. What did she have but time? She was crossing 23rd Street and thinking about a children's clothing store in the neighborhood that she might peek into when "Jingle Bells" blared so loudly from within her coat that she jumped, nearly stumbling over an indignant dachshund being walked by an elderly man.

"Sorry! I'm sorry!" exclaimed Allie as she fumbled for her phone. To her surprise, since she thought she had set the volume as high as it would go, the sounds of "Jingle Bells" grew even louder (and somewhat frantic) as she struggled to unbutton her coat and reach into the pocket.

She didn't bother to check the caller ID. "Hello? Hello?" she said breathlessly.

"Hi! It's me!" said the voice at the other end of the line. "Did the baby come yet?"

"Ruby?" asked Aunt Allie.

"Yup. And Flora's here, too. We just wanted to know if we have a new cousin."

"Oh, believe me, honey, you two and Min are the

first people I'll call when there's any news, but I haven't heard from Mrs. Prescott today."

"Oh." Ruby paused. "For corn's sake! That's what Min would say."

Allie laughed. "I know. Listen, I promise I'll call you the moment anything happens. But it's nice to hear your voice. I'm sorry I'm going to miss your solos tomorrow."

"Me, too. But you'll get to hear me in the Christmas concert. Just wait. It's the longest and best solo I've ever — What? But I'm right in the middle of —" Allie heard a muffled commotion on the other end of the line, and then Ruby said, "Oh, *okay*. Aunt Allie, Flora wants to talk to you."

"Hi, Aunt Allie! We just wanted to tell you we're thinking about you," said Flora. "And our cousin, of course. We'll talk to you again soon."

"Thanks for calling, honey." Allie clicked off her phone, but not before she heard Flora say, "Ruby, not everything is about *you*. We were calling to talk about the baby, not your solos."

Allie smiled as she continued along Fifth Avenue. She decided not to look in the children's clothing store and instead marched resolutely north toward Midtown. At last, she glimpsed a long line of people snaking back and forth in front of brightly lit windows. She had reached Lord & Taylor — and what she personally considered to be the most splendid windows in the entire city. Allie joined the line. In front of her were two women and two little girls. The girls were about six and four, Allie guessed, dressed in woolen mittens and woolen scarves and woolen leg warmers and woolen hats. The younger one kept tugging at her mother's hand and saying, "But I don't see Santa anywhere!"

"This isn't the line for Santa," said the older girl patiently. "This is the line for the windows. Look. We're almost there."

"But I want to see Santa!"

"But you can't."

"But I want to!"

Once again, Allie jumped when her coat began to play "Jingle Bells," but this time she answered her phone more quickly. "Hello?" she said breathlessly, and the small girl turned around to stare at her. Allie's heart was pounding. Please be Mrs. Prescott, she pleaded silently.

"Allie? This is Gigi."

Allie sagged slightly but managed to say, "Gigi! What a surprise."

"Any news yet? Min told me what's going on. Actually, she's told everyone what's going on. I just had to give you a call."

"Thank you," said Allie. "Well, nothing's happening. Nothing new, anyway. I haven't heard from Mrs. Prescott today and that means the birth mother hasn't gone into labor yet. Which is what the doctors want."

"This must be so nerve-wracking," said Gigi. "All right. I won't keep you."

Allie put her phone away again, and the line continued to snake toward the windows. Allie inched along with it. She was standing on tiptoe, trying to peer around a tall man wearing a hat, when, for the third time, "Jingle Bells" blared from her coat. Allie was prepared and whisked the phone out expertly, clicking the ON button before two seconds had passed.

Please be Mrs. Prescott.

"Hello?" said Allie.

"Hello?" said a shaky voice.

"Mr. Pennington?"

"Allie?"

"Yes, it's me. Hello!"

"Where am I reaching you? Min told me this is your cell phone number and, well, you could be anywhere."

Allie laughed. "I'm on Fifth Avenue, standing in line to see the windows at Lord and Taylor."

"My, my," said Mr. Pennington. He paused. "I guess this means there isn't any news yet."

"No." Allie sighed. "Not yet . . . Um, Mr. Pennington? Could you please hold for a minute? I'm getting another call." Allie pressed a button on her phone and crossed her fingers. "Hello?" she said.

Please be Mrs. Prescott.

"Allie? Hi, honey!"

"Oh, my goodness!" exclaimed Allie when she heard Min's voice. "Mr. Pennington is on the other line. And Gigi has called, and Ruby and Flora have called. There's no news."

"Well, I swan," said Min. "I'm sorry. Call me later, okay?"

"Okay."

Allie finished her call with Mr. Pennington just as she reached the first window. She gratefully dropped the phone back in her pocket and gazed at the scene before her. It was a nursery — it could have been the Darling children's nursery in *Peter Pan* — decorated for Christmas. A pair of black boots was dangling down the chimney and hovering above the hearth, and the children in their beds kept sitting up and pointing to the boots with as much excitement as mechanical boys and girls could muster.

Allie was trying to take in every detail of the window when she heard the first notes of "Jingle Bells" from her pocket. She grabbed the phone, almost laughing. "Hello?"

"Allie? This is Mrs. Prescott."

For one brief instant, Allie thought she might faint. She stepped away from the crowd of people, not caring that she lost her place in the long line. "Mrs. Prescott?" she whispered.

"I just heard from the hospital. The birth mother went into labor again after all."

Allie drew in her breath. "Is that bad news?"

"Well, of course it would have been better if the baby could have waited a bit longer, but," Mrs. Prescott paused, "but I don't think this is bad news."

"Okay."

"Now it's a matter of more waiting. I'll keep you posted. I'll call you every time I have an update."

Allie leaned against a lamppost. She thanked Mrs. Prescott and immediately phoned Min. "The baby is on its way," she said, but she was so close to tears that Min couldn't hear what she'd said and she had to repeat herself.

"Oh, my," said Min. "My stars and garters. I'll spread the word."

"Thank you," whispered Allie. She put her phone away, and now the tears spilled as she stood on Fifth Avenue, sniffling and wiping her eyes and searching for a tissue.

"Mommy," said the little girl who wanted to see Santa Claus. "Look. That lady is crying."

"They're happy tears!" Allie called to the girl, and she turned and headed back downtown to the apartment.

CHAPTER 8

Wednesday Afternoon and Evening, November 25ᵗʰ

"Vacation, vacation! I love vacation!" chanted Ruby. "If I were a poet, I would write an ode to vacation. Or maybe I should write a song about it."

"Vacation is pretty wonderful," agreed Flora. She and Ruby were lying end-to-end on the couch in the living room of the Row House, King Comma perched precariously on their knees, Daisy Dear on the floor.

"I could spend the next four days doing nothing but this," said Ruby with a sigh. "We didn't even get any homework today."

"We did," said Flora. "Oh, well."

The phone rang then and Ruby said lazily, "Let's just let the machine answer it."

"No. It might be Min," said Flora. "She'll worry if we don't pick up." She passed off King Comma, staggered to her feet, and reached for the phone. "Hello?"

"Are you ready to become a cousin?"

"Min?" cried Flora. "What do you mean? We talked to Aunt Allie half an hour ago and —"

"Mrs. Prescott just called her. The birth mother's in labor."

"Ruby!" shrieked Flora. "The baby's coming!"

Ruby let out a shriek of her own. "Oh, my lord in heaven! I hope it's a boy! I want a boy cousin!"

"But Aunt Allie only has girl things," Flora shouted, and then realized that she was shouting into Min's ear. "Sorry," she said.

On the other end of the phone, Min was laughing. "It is exciting, isn't it? Anyway, I just wanted to let you know. I'll see you and Ruby later."

Flora clicked off the phone, sat on the couch, staring at nothing, and then announced, "I have a great idea."

"Just like that?" asked Ruby.

"Just like that. Okay. Here it is. You and Min and I should secretly get the nursery ready in case Aunt Allie brings the baby home when she comes back from New York. It would be a great surprise for her."

"Maybe the room is already ready," said Ruby.

"No, it isn't. You didn't see a nursery over there the last time we visited, did you?"

"Well, no."

"Exactly. Now. Aunt Allie has three bedrooms — her room, our room, and the guest room. So she must be planning to turn the guest room into the nursery.

Boy, she has a lot of work to do. That's why we should do it for her."

"Yeah . . ." said Ruby slowly. "We could take all the stuff out of that weird baby supply closet and arrange it in the room."

"Also, we should baby-proof the house. I'd better call Min. We ought to get started right away." Flora picked up the phone and dialed Needle and Thread.

Min answered, and when Flora explained her idea, Min exclaimed, "Oh, honey! How lovely. Aunt Allie will be very touched. Listen, Gigi and I are going to close the store early today anyway. So let me finish things here, and then I'll stop at the hardware store to pick up a few items. I'll be home as soon as I can."

"This is going to be so great," said Flora rapturously. "And fun. I'm dying to fix up the nursery!"

"But we can't do everything," Ruby pointed out. "We don't have paint or wallpaper. And, hey, we don't have a crib or a changing table or any of the big stuff."

Flora considered this. "Maybe Aunt Allie has them somewhere but she hasn't set them up yet. Just like she hasn't put out the clothes."

"Maybe," said Ruby dubiously.

"But probably not. Gosh, I wonder if we could borrow them before we leave for New York. Aunt Allie can*not* bring the baby home to a guest room."

"She's probably not going to be bringing the baby home on Sunday anyway, you know."

"I know." And even as Flora said this, an uneasy thought surfaced in her mind. What if the birth parents decided to keep the baby? This was *their* baby, after all. Allie had said they might change their minds. That was why there was a waiting period after the birth. "Ruby," Flora started to say.

But Ruby was gazing dreamily out the window and hadn't heard her sister. "What do you think we should name the baby?" she asked.

"*We?* What about Aunt Allie?"

Ruby shrugged. "I'm sure she'll be open to suggestions. Now, I've been thinking, and I've decided that the perfect name is Douglas."

"That isn't perfect for a girl," Flora pointed out.

"But if Aunt Allie doesn't like it," Ruby continued, "then I'd agree to Franklin. Or Pablo! What about Pablo?"

"Hey, I have a question. What if the baby is a girl?"

Ruby waved her hand impatiently. "Girls' names are a dime a dozen."

"What on earth are you talking about?" asked Flora.

"I actually have no idea. I just want a boy."

"Well, I think we should be prepared for a girl. And if that happens, I hope Aunt Allie likes the name Whitney."

"For a *girl?*"

"It's a very trendy girl's name," said Flora with dignity.

"Whatever happened to Susan? Or Emily or Sarah or . . . hey, Theresa is a nice name. We could call her Terry for short."

"Huh," said Flora. "Not bad. But what about something a little more glamorous? Like Lily Sophia? Or Marilee Rose?"

"Steven," said Ruby.

"Augustania," said Flora.

They were still discussing names when they heard a voice at the front door calling, "Hello? Girls?"

Flora and Ruby jumped up from the couch and made a dash for the hallway.

"Flora wants to name the baby Augustania!" wailed Ruby before Min had even removed her coat.

"Ruby will only consider boys' names!" exclaimed Flora.

"Don't you think you're putting the cart before the horse?" was Min's reply.

"What?" said Ruby.

"She means we're getting ahead of ourselves," said Flora, sounding maddeningly superior.

"So before I hear another word about names, let's concentrate on your wonderful idea." Min hung up her coat and held out a bag from Zack's hardware store. "Look in here."

Ruby whisked the bag out of Min's hands and swung it away from Flora. She peered inside. "What is all this?"

Flora grabbed the bag from Ruby. "*I* know what it is," she exclaimed, pawing through the contents. "This is stuff for baby-proofing the house. You fasten these locks to cabinet doors so the baby can't get into cleaning supplies and medicine. And you put these covers over electrical outlets so the baby can't stick his fingers —"

"*His!* You said *his!*" crowed Ruby. "You secretly think the baby is going to be a boy. You just won't admit it."

"For the love of Mike." Min took the bag from Flora and set it by the front door. "I don't know what's gotten into you two, but if you don't calm down and start talking to each other like sisters instead of like cavemen" (Ruby resisted pointing out that she didn't think cavemen had had much of a language system, and in any case she would be a cave*woman*) "then you may not come with me to Allie's. Now, the two of you had a lovely idea" (here Flora resisted pointing out that it was her idea alone) "and we could have a lot of fun carrying it out. But not unless you can be pleasant. So. I am about to get in the car. You are welcome to join me. Are you going to come along and be the agreeable girls I ate breakfast with this morning? Or shall I drop you off at Mr. Pennington's on my way to Allie's?"

"Sorry, Min," said Flora. "I want to go with you."

"Sorry, Min," echoed Ruby. "I want to go, too."

"All right."

Twenty minutes later, Min, Flora, and Ruby were standing in the guest room on the second floor of Aunt Allie's house.

"I *guess* this is going to be the baby's room," said Flora.

"Unless she turns *our* room into the nursery," said Ruby in a small voice.

"No," said Min firmly. "I know that the room she fixed up for you is not to be changed. But after the baby arrives, it might be used as the guest room from time to time." Min clapped her hands together. "Well, the first thing we should do is try to move the furniture out of here. We can put it in the attic."

"But what about furniture for the baby?" asked Ruby. "We were talking about that before you came home. Does Aunt Allie have a crib or anything?"

"I don't think so," replied Min. "But I'll bet we can borrow the essentials until Allie buys things of her own. I'll start making some phone calls. You never know what people may have saved. I think I'll start with the Morrises. They probably have some furniture stowed in their attic."

"Or their basement," said Ruby knowledgeably, thinking of the Malones' basement.

Flora and Ruby set to work in the guest room.

"We can take the bed apart. I think I know how to do that," said Flora. "The headboard should come off. All we need is a screwdriver. It isn't going to be easy to carry the mattress and the box spring down the hall to the attic, though."

"But I bet we can do it," said Ruby. "We can carry the dresser, too. It isn't that big."

Flora and Ruby had managed to disassemble the bed and carry most of it into the attic by the time Min came hurrying up the stairs. "This is wonderful," she said. "The Morrises still have their crib and a changing table, the Fongs have a Diaper Genie that they aren't using for some reason, and if you can believe it, Mrs. Edwards says she has Robby's dresser from when he was a baby."

"I can believe it," said Ruby.

"Everyone is going to bring the things over now." Min paused. "I wish we had time to buy some clothes for the baby. Maybe I should phone Mrs. Fong back. Maybe she could lend us some of Grace's things."

Flora and Ruby exchanged a glance, and Flora said, "I don't really think you need to do that."

Min frowned. "Why not?"

"Well, we didn't tell you this," said Ruby, "but a couple of months ago, we found something." She took Min's hand and tugged her down the hallway to the closet. "I wasn't snooping when I opened this door. Honest!" (Ruby neglected to mention the sleuthing she'd done later.) "We felt like this was a secret of Aunt Allie's, so we didn't tell you . . ." Her voice trailed off.

Min put her arm around Ruby. "You did the right thing," was all she said. And then, "Goodness me! There's practically an entire department store in here! I think it's high time this closet was emptied out."

Flora felt her spirits lift. She and Ruby and Min

carried armloads of baby clothes and supplies into the nursery. The doorbell rang as their neighbors began to arrive with the furniture — and with other things they had found. The Fongs brought a framed picture of a kitten as well as the Diaper Genie. Mrs. Edwards brought along a few of Robby's old picture books. And Mr. Morris arrived with a rocking chair in addition to the other furniture.

Min bustled around, arranging and rearranging the furniture with the help of Mr. Morris. Flora and Ruby tucked tiny shirts and blankets and socks and bibs into the drawers of the dresser.

"I think," said Ruby, standing back at last to admire their efforts, "that this is going to be the perfect room for Maxwell."

"Maxwell? What happened to Douglas?"

"Nothing. I'm just considering my options."

"Well, *I* think it's the perfect room for Honoria."

"Scott."

"Calpurnia."

"James."

"Kate."

"David."

"Emma."

"Girls," said Min. She eyed them sternly and whispered, "Cavemen."

Ruby turned to Flora and whispered, "Cave*women*," and Flora began to giggle helplessly.

CHAPTER 9

Thanksgiving Morning, November 26th

Mary Woolsey buttoned her bathrobe as she padded into her kitchen. She could hear Daphne and Delilah padding along behind her, and she turned to them and smiled. "Funny old girls," she said. "Actually, if we're going to be honest, you two are decrepit old girls. In cat years, you're at least a hundred and five."

Daphne opened her mouth and yawned, as if this bit of information bored her tremendously.

"Happy Thanksgiving," added Mary. "Look what a beautiful day it is." She peered out the window and into her backyard. Frost glittered on the stone wall, on the stubbly remains of her gardens, on every blade of grass, even on the woodpile. "A perfect sunrise," said Mary, looking to the sky. The clouds that skittered along behind the trees had turned a bright pink, the color of the hyacinths that, years ago, Mary had planted by her front door.

"Come look, girls." Mary held first Daphne, then

Delilah, up to the window. Daphne squirmed from her grasp, but Delilah appeared to scan the yard and sky appreciatively.

Mary started the coffeemaker and then turned her attention to the cats' breakfast. She spooned wet food into identical pink dishes, the bottoms of which were adorned with the letter D. The dishes were a tiny extravagance Mary had allowed herself one day. Money was scarce, but Mary had never had to borrow a penny, not once in all the years of her long life. Her mother had taught her to budget and to live within her means, and Mary had learned the lessons well.

She was about to fix her own breakfast when her eyes fell on the basket in the center of her dining table. A smile crossed her face as she remembered the previous afternoon.

"Mary?" Min Read had called from the checkout counter at Needle and Thread. "Gigi and I are going to close up early for the holiday. Why don't you go home? You can have a nice long evening if you leave now."

"Thank you," replied Mary, and she had begun to tidy up her worktable.

"You're sure you won't join us at Three Oaks tomorrow?" asked Min. "There's room for one more at the Willets' table."

"Thank you," said Mary again. "But I think I'll stay at home." The idea of eating in a dining room the size of the one at Three Oaks had made her breath catch in her throat.

"You're welcome to join *us*," added Gigi. "It's our big family celebration. We're a little on the noisy side, but . . ."

Mary smiled and shook her head. "I appreciate the offers. I really do."

Gigi had looked expectantly at her old friend, but Mary said nothing further. She pulled on her coat.

"Happy Thanksgiving, then," said Gigi.

"Happy Thanksgiving to you. Bye, Min," added Mary as the telephone began to ring.

Min, still at the checkout counter, smiled and waved and reached for the phone. As Mary slipped out the door, she heard Min say, "Allie? Is that you? What was that?" And then, "My stars and garters. I'll spread the word."

Mary made her way through the darkening streets of Camden Falls. She had always liked the day before a holiday, the hours when the town was still expectant and excitement buzzed in the air. As she'd passed houses, lights flicked on, shades were pulled down, children sprinted onto porches and burst through doorways. She'd watched a UPS driver hop out of his van and hurry along the path to a small house where the door was flung open and a man exclaimed, "Oh, wonderful! I've been waiting for this!"

Mary paused, smiling. How thrilling it would be to answer her bell one day and find the UPS driver waiting there with a box for her — a surprise birthday package, maybe.

Mary turned the corner to her street, admiring the wreath of chrysanthemums that hung on the Lewises' lamppost and the pumpkins that still marched up the steps to the Golds' house. She walked through the gardens, now brittle and brown, to her cottage, grateful for the streetlights that lit her way, and had unlocked her door and swung it open before she noticed the basket at her feet.

"What's this?" she said aloud, and stooped to pick it up. A card was attached to the handle of the basket, but she couldn't make out the writing in the dim light, so she carried the basket inside, feeling every bit as lucky as the man who had received his UPS package.

Mary turned on a light and set her pocketbook on the floor. She sat in an armchair and admired the basket. It was made of wicker and lined with a soft dishcloth. She reached for the card again. It read, *Happy Thanksgiving, Mary!*

Mary turned the card over. That was it. Nothing on the back.

"Well, it *is* a happy Thanksgiving," said Mary.

She turned her attention to the contents of the basket. A bouquet of delicate dried flowers had been arranged on one side. Nestled among brightly colored maple leaves were a small cardboard box, a cellophane bag containing cookies, and a pair of candles shaped like a Pilgrim girl and a Pilgrim boy.

Mary reached for the box and withdrew it from the leaves. She sniffed. "Chocolate," she said with pleasure, and opened the lid. Sure enough, six chocolate candies were inside. Mary replaced the box and opened the bag. "Gingersnaps. How lovely. Look, girls," she'd added as Delilah and Daphne jumped onto the arm of the chair. "A Thanksgiving surprise. But who is it from?"

Now in the pale light of Thanksgiving morning, Mary looked fondly at the basket again. She had several thoughts about who might have sent it, but she was enjoying the mystery and didn't really want to solve it.

The morning unfolded in the slow, delicious way of holidays. Mary began to prepare her solitary Thanksgiving dinner. She lit a fire in the fireplace. She put a small turkey in the oven, promising Delilah and Daphne that they would get samples with their suppers that evening. She had just fixed a pot of tea when her doorbell rang.

"Now, who could that be?" Mary asked Daphne, who was sitting on the kitchen counter. She wiped her hands on her apron and made her way to the front door. "Flora!" she exclaimed.

"Happy Thanksgiving!" cried Flora.

"What a surprise! Come in. I just made tea. Can you stay?"

"Long enough for tea," replied Flora. "I have to meet Min and Mr. Pennington at the community center soon. But guess what. The baby is on the way! Aunt Allie's baby."

Mary clasped her hands together.

"It will probably be born today," Flora went on. "And Ruby and I will have a new cousin, and Min will be a grandmother again, and Aunt Allie will be a mom. And we can stop calling the baby 'it.'"

Mary laughed. "What a wonderful way to celebrate Thanksgiving."

Flora left half an hour later, and Mary decided to read before the fire for a while. Early in the afternoon, she sat down to her turkey dinner, which she ate with two cats staring intently at her. "I told you I was going to give you turkey tonight," Mary reminded them, and then fed them bites of turkey anyway.

She was clearing her dishes when the telephone rang. "Min," said Mary to herself. It could only be Min. She picked up the phone. "Happy Thanksgiving!"

There was a brief pause at the other end of the line before an unfamiliar voice said, "Well, happy Thanksgiving. Is this . . . is this Mary Woolsey?"

"Yes," said Mary. "Who's this?"

"Well, you don't know me. I mean, you sent me a letter. . . ." The voice trailed off. "My name is Catherine? Catherine Landry?"

Mary frowned. The name sounded familiar. "Catherine."

"Yes. Well, the thing is, I think we're related."

Mary dropped onto one of the kitchen chairs. "Oh," she said, and her voice came out as a squeak.

"I didn't mean to take you by surprise, but you did write —"

"Yes. Yes, of course."

"And I'm pretty certain that I'm your half sister."

"My *half sister*," Mary repeated. "I thought maybe cousins or . . ."

Mary remembered the day the previous summer when she'd found the courage to write the letter. She had recently learned the truth about her father — that he had a sister, for one thing, and more important, that he had not died young, as she had believed for most of her life, but instead had left Mary and her mother and started a new life somewhere far from Camden Falls. Mary had been brought up believing that she had no relatives at all, and then she had discovered that her father had had a sister. That sister might have children — they would be Mary's cousins. But *this* — a sister of her own — this was more than Mary had hoped for.

Catherine was speaking again. "I know this must be a shock. Your letter was sent along to me by someone who knew your aunt, our father's sister, decades ago. Probably fifty years ago. I gather you were trying to find out about your aunt's family. I'm sorry to tell you that she died in, I think it was nineteen sixty."

"Excuse me for interrupting," said Mary, "but I have to ask you this: Did you know that your father — I mean, our father — had been married before?"

"I didn't find out until after he died," replied Catherine. "And I had so little information that I didn't know how to find you. But then you found me."

Mary drew in her breath. "Do we have any other sisters or brothers?" she whispered.

Catherine began to talk again. The minutes ticked by. An hour passed. Mary had a brother. She had nieces and nephews. And she did indeed have cousins as well. The pieces of her life, all the missing pieces, were falling into place. Mary asked questions and Catherine answered them. Catherine asked questions and Mary answered them.

Catherine lived less than an hour away. Two of Mary's nephews lived even closer.

Mary closed her eyes. "Could we meet?" she asked.

"I was hoping you would say that!" exclaimed Catherine. "Yes. Yes, I would very much like to meet."

"I haven't left Camden Falls in years," admitted Mary. "I don't even have a car. Do you think you could come here?"

"Not only that, I'll come with my sons, my daughter, and my niece. *And* my granddaughter," she added proudly. "Ellen Hayley. She's two months old."

"Goodness!" said Mary.

She had never known such a Thanksgiving. When she finally hung up the phone, she wandered into the kitchen and caught sight of the mysterious basket.

"You brought me luck," she said to it. "You must be magic." And for the rest of the day she eyed it both gratefully and suspiciously.

CHAPTER 10

Thanksgiving Morning, November 26ᵗʰ

Ruby Northrop woke up on Thanksgiving morning with the uncomfortable feeling that she had forgotten something. Or that she had lost something. She sat up and looked around her room. She didn't see any schoolbooks, but that was okay because she hadn't been given any vacation homework. She saw her tap shoes, which was good because they were very expensive and Min had told her that if she lost them again, Ruby would have to replace them herself.

What could be wrong?

The answer came to her in the next instant and left a sinking feeling in her stomach.

She had forgotten to rehearse her solos (the little one *and* the important one) for the Thanksgiving concert. She had missed the final rehearsal and she had forgotten to rehearse on her own.

"Oh, well," said Ruby aloud, hopping out of bed. She pulled her sheet music out from under a pile of papers on her desk, unwrapped a piece of bubble gum, popped it in her mouth, and scanned the music. "I know this," she said. She snapped her gum and dropped the music back on the desk. Nothing to worry about. Not to mention that this was Ruby's *second* Thanksgiving concert with the Children's Chorus.

"Been there, done that," said Ruby, and she opened her wardrobe to choose an outfit for Thanksgiving dinner at Three Oaks.

The concert was to begin at ten o'clock in the morning in order to give everyone plenty of time to tend to their feasts afterward. The members of the Children's Chorus were to arrive at the community center at nine-fifteen sharp, wearing white tops and navy skirts or pants. And they were not to have their sheet music with them. The concerts were traditionally given from memory. No music allowed.

Ruby was just a teensy bit anxious about not having her music. She thought back to the previous Thanksgiving concert, which had been her very first concert with the chorus. She had not had a solo then — none of the brand-new members had been given one. But this concert was different. Ruby was now a second-year member.

Feeling quite responsible and grown-up, Ruby had laid a green velvet dress out on her bed that morning. It was to be her outfit for Three Oaks. Then she had reached for the white blouse and navy skirt that were hanging, freshly pressed by Min, in her wardrobe. She put them on carefully. They remained wrinkle free. And Ruby was quite pleased that she had had the forethought to lay out her dress ahead of time so she wouldn't have to worry about an outfit later.

"I'm all organized," Ruby announced to Flora and Min when she entered the kitchen that morning. "I'm ready for the concert, and I chose my outfit for this afternoon. So in case we don't have much time after the concert, I can get dressed really fast."

"That's admirable, Ruby," said Min. "I'm proud of you."

"Now, if I can just eat breakfast without spilling anything," said Ruby.

"Why don't you wear a bib?" suggested Flora.

"Ha-ha," said Ruby. "Min, who's going to drive Lacey and me to the community center?"

"I am. We should leave at nine o'clock, okay?"

"Okay."

Min looked at her watch. "It's quarter to eight now. You'll have time to practice your solos before we leave."

Ruby removed her wad of bubble gum and stuck it on the edge of her plate. "Don't need to. I'm ready."

"I haven't heard any rehearsing."

Ruby shrugged. "We're singing these songs from the nineteen forties — I'm not sure why —"

"Didn't Ms. Angelo explain why she chose the songs for the concert?" interrupted Flora.

"Yes. I mean, she must have," said Ruby dubiously. "Well, anyway, both of my solos are in 'Boogie Woogie Bugle Boy.' That's a song made famous by the Andrews Sisters. First I have just one line, but at the end I have —"

"I still didn't hear you rehearsing," said Min.

Ruby squirmed in her seat. "These are really tasty sticky buns," she remarked.

Min sighed. "Be ready by nine."

At exactly nine-fifteen, Ruby and Lacey arrived at the community center. The outside air, which was very cold, smelled of fallen leaves and wood smoke and pine needles. The sky was clear and blue.

"Remember last year?" said Ruby. "Remember how beautiful the community center looked during the concert?"

Ruby hadn't known, when she'd entered the center the previous Thanksgiving, that the spare wooden hall, which was vast and dim, would be decorated for the holiday, or that the room would be infused with color and warmth. Now she opened the door eagerly and peered inside.

"Yes!" she exclaimed under her breath. She was pleased to see that pots of live chrysanthemums had been placed at the ends of the first four rows of seats and that large gourds tumbled from a bushel basket at each side of the risers, on which the members of the chorus would stand. Around the windows were looped ropes of greens, and bouquets of lush red and orange and yellow flowers stood at either side of the doors. The room once again felt warm and cozy and festive.

Ms. Angelo, the chorus director, clapped her hands. "Good morning, everyone!" she called. "Happy Thanksgiving. I know you're excited, but please take your places on the risers for one quick rehearsal before the concert begins."

Ruby and her friends warmed up, rehearsed the two most difficult pieces (which did not include "Boogie Woogie Bugle Boy"), and practiced filing into and out of the hall and finding their spots on the risers.

"Remember," said Ms. Angelo, smiling, "we are not elephants. Please enter as quietly as possible. Without actually tiptoeing, of course."

By ten o'clock, when Ms. Angelo and the chorus were waiting patiently outside the great hall, almost every seat had been filled. Ruby could hear hushed, happy voices, and she tried to picture Min and Flora and Mr. Pennington sitting in a row near the front, dressed in their best clothes. The Morrises would be there, too, and maybe Olivia and her family. She wished Aunt Allie could hear her solos, but then she thought of the baby (please be a boy, please be a boy) and felt a shiver of pleasure run along her back.

"Children," said Ms. Angelo, after peeking through the doors, "it's time. Are you ready?"

The members of the chorus fell into place behind

the director and followed her into the assembly room, which was now silent. Ruby breathed in the scent of the flowers and thought about "Boogie Woogie Bugle Boy." When she was standing in her spot on the risers, she looked out at the expectant faces and almost immediately found Mr. Pennington, her grandmother, and her sister. They smiled discreetly at her. She looked around and spotted Lacey's family, Olivia and her family, and then saw Nikki, Tobias, Mae, and their mother. She caught sight of Frank, the owner of Frank's Beans, and Jackie from the post office, and other people from stores and businesses up and down Main Street.

This was great, thought Ruby. The whole town had turned out to hear her solos.

Ms. Angelo faced the audience, smiled warmly at them, and said, "Welcome to our Thanksgiving concert. We're pleased that so many of you are here this morning, celebrating our day for giving thanks. The Camden Falls Children's Chorus has been working hard this fall, and we're eager to share our music with you. We thank you for coming and hope you enjoy the program."

Ms. Angelo turned back to the chorus. She nodded once, played a single note on the piano, and raised her hands. This was when Ruby suddenly recalled that not only was no sheet music allowed, but the singers were to have memorized the order of the songs to be performed. So she was a beat late getting started since she couldn't remember whether the first song was "When the Lights Go On Again" or "Sentimental Journey." Lacey, who was standing to her left, glanced curiously at her, but once the song was under way, Ruby was fine.

She felt so fine, in fact, that she couldn't help but notice that others were not quite fine. The altos, for example, seemed just the teeniest bit off-key. And Germaine Lasley, who was standing behind Ruby, kept saying "No Peeking" instead of "Topeka" when they sang the song about the railroads. Germaine had a loud, although lovely, voice, and Ruby found it disconcerting to hear "On the Atchison, No Peeking, and the Santa Fe!" bleating into her ears.

The chorus took a brief break after the fourth song. Ruby glanced at Lacey. "Did you hear the altos?" she whispered.

Lacey frowned. "*I'm* an alto," she reminded her.

"Well, *you* weren't flat," said Ruby hastily.

"You thought the altos were flat?"

"Um," said Ruby. And then she couldn't help herself. She turned around and hissed to Germaine, "It's To-pe-ka. Not No Peeking. To. Pe. Ka."

"Sor-*ry*," said Germaine.

"Some people just can't take criticism," Ruby whispered to Lacey.

Ms. Angelo raised her arm for attention then, and the members of the chorus as well as everyone in the audience fell silent.

Ruby realized that once again she didn't know

which song came next, so she kept her mouth closed for the first few notes. She was surprised to discover that her friends were singing "Boogie Woogie Bugle Boy." Here would be not only her solo line but many others, since the kids were to take turns singing. It was a song full of solos. Ruby drew in her breath and then caught up. The kids sang the first verse as a group. Then suddenly Lacey was singing alone next to Ruby. Germaine had the next line, followed by a sixth-grade boy, and then a girl whose name Ruby could never remember. What on earth was it? Either Jenny or Jeanie, Ruby decided. Or possibly Penny.

Ruby was just thinking that perhaps the girl's name was Janice when she realized the room was silent. The entire room. Not a single voice was to be heard. The song couldn't be over, could it? Ruby hadn't sung her solo line. Then she saw that Ms. Angelo was looking sternly in her direction. At the same time, she felt Lacey pinch her side. "It's your turn!" whispered Lacey as loudly as she dared.

Ruby gasped. Then she opened her mouth and sang, *"He's in the army now, a-blowin' reveille."* She paused, not sure where her part ended, and decided to continue. *"He's the boogie woogie —"*

"Stop!" hissed Lacey.

And Ruby realized that Jordan Banks was singing, *"He's the boogie woogie bugle boy of Company B,"* glaring fiercely at her as he did so.

Ruby's face was flaming. She listened to the voices as they continued around her. She knew the song. She just wasn't quite sure about the division of the lines for the solos. She did remember — and just in time — that she was to sing the entire last verse by herself. That was her main solo, the one she'd been looking forward to. It went off without a hitch.

The concert continued. Each time a new song began, Ruby had to wait a beat or two to find out what it was before she could join in. When the final line of "Sweet Slumber" hung in the air, Ms. Angelo turned to the audience, smiled, and said simply, "Thank you."

The audience erupted into applause, but Ruby knew it wasn't for her. She looked at her feet as she filed out of the room, and then she made a mad dash for Min.

"Min! Min!" she cried, and she ran into her grandmother's arms. "Let's go home right now!"

Min, Flora, and Mr. Pennington were still shrugging into their coats and edging out of their row of seats.

"I'm sorry you're upset," said Min, and tried to disengage herself from Ruby and button her coat at the same time.

But Ruby buried her face against Min's coat, not so much for comfort but because she sensed that Ms. Angelo might be in search of her. She tugged at her grandmother. "Please, let's just go."

Mr. Pennington peeked at his watch and said, "We really should be on our way. The concert lasted a little longer than I expected."

Flora refrained from saying, "Probably because Ruby took so long to start singing." Instead, she slipped an arm around her sister's shoulders.

Ruby, gripping Min's coat, hustled out of the community center before Ms. Angelo could speak to her.

CHAPTER II

Thanksgiving Morning, November 26th

Willow Hamilton stood at the base of a circular staircase that wound from the third floor to the fourth floor. In the lobby, which now seemed very far below, the staircase was stunning, but even up here it was impressive, with a wide, highly polished mahogany banister and a lavender-and-green carpet held in place at the back of each step by a shiny brass rod. Lovely. Willow tipped her head back and looked up. How many more floors did this place have? she wondered.

Deer Lodge, it was called. When her father had first mentioned it to her and Cole, she had pictured a cabin in the woods, and probably not a cabin she would like much — one featuring the heads of slain animals on the walls, their fur as rugs on the floors, and displays of rifles and arrows and other instruments of torture. Hunting was wrong, senseless, useless, and cruel, and now her father was going to make her spend this

Thanksgiving, which was already horrible, in a place called Deer Lodge.

Willow should have known better. She should have known that her father, wanting only to give her and her brother a pleasant break from the sadness in their lives, wouldn't take them to a place with reminders of death in every room. And he hadn't. Deer Lodge, commanding a striking view from its New England mountaintop, had turned out to be the grandest hotel Willow had ever seen. It was enormous and sprawling, and every inch was beautiful. Willow felt like a princess in a palace. Best of all, her father had said on that first morning, Thanksgiving morning, that she and Cole were free to explore the hotel on their own.

Leaving their father ensconced in an armchair in the lobby, with the newspaper and a cup of coffee at his elbow, Willow and Cole had set off, basking in their independence and also in the sense that around any corner they might stumble across a mystery. But almost immediately, they had discovered a game room, and Cole had settled in. "This is where I'm going to spend the morning," he had announced. "Look at all these cool old games."

Willow had tried not to look disappointed. "Couldn't we explore just a little bit?" she had asked.

"Oh, you can go explore. I don't mind."

"But how are you going to play games all by yourself?"

"Well, I need to study some of them first," Cole replied seriously. "I haven't even heard of that one," he said, pointing. "Or that one. And anyway, I'll bet some other kids will come along and then I can play with them. Just tell Dad where I am, okay?"

"Okay," Willow said, and realized that she was quite happy at the prospect of exploring on her own. All at once, it seemed like exactly the right kind of thing for this particular morning — a morning of promise and novelty and old secrets.

So Willow dashed back to the lobby and told her father that Cole was down the hall in the game room, and then with a great sense of purpose she climbed the circular staircase to the second floor. At the top she looked right and left along the corridor, which was carpeted in the same green and lavender as the stairs. Just rooms? she wondered. Did something other than plain old hotel rooms lie behind any of these doors? She turned left and wandered through the hallway, noticing that the floor creaked pleasingly beneath her feet. Was she in a castle? In an imposing hotel in London? Had she traveled back in time? Anything seemed possible.

Willow walked all the way to the end of the corridor and found that she could continue to the left — down another long corridor lined with doors. So far, she had seen nothing but room numbers on the doors and was just beginning to feel a bit disappointed when she came to a door that was open. She peeked inside and found a parlor overlooking a lawn, scrubby and brown in the November cold, that rolled away to a pine-dotted mountain slope. A sitting room, thought Willow. And she decided to sit and think. She chose an overstuffed floral chair facing the window. The arms and the back of the chair were draped with lace doilies the color of weak tea. Beside the chair, an ornate table held two books, a delicate lamp, and a pitcher. Willow looked in the pitcher. It was empty, but across the room a table with wheels held an immaculate silver tea service, and Willow wondered if a real afternoon tea might be served here later. She imagined herself sipping tea as, on the other side of the windows, shadows fell and the mountains dissolved in blackness.

Willow relaxed into the chair. She felt as far away from her old home, as far away from Camden Falls, as far away from her mother — as far away from her life — as she ever had, and she liked that. She wouldn't say that living with her mother had been torture; that would be an exaggeration. But living with her mother had been difficult and confusing and sometimes very, very scary. Her mother was mentally ill. That much Willow understood. She didn't, however, know exactly what was wrong with her mother and had recently decided that it didn't matter. What mattered was that her mother was in the hospital again, and maybe this time she would truly get better. What mattered was that Willow and Cole could get on with their lives in a more normal fashion. What mattered was that Willow and Cole and their father could try to make their Row House into a real home.

Willow let out a sigh. After her mother had gone to the hospital, as horrible as that night had been, Willow had felt that instead of a hole in the family, her mother's absence had at last made the family whole.

How awful that sounded. And yet, that was how Willow felt. Most of the time. But strangely not today. Today, Willow wished for her mother; she wished for a mom and a dad and a sister and a brother gathered around the table before their Thanksgiving dinner.

Willow recalled a conversation she had had with her father a week earlier. She had been sitting in the kitchen finishing her homework, Cole already asleep upstairs, and her father had turned on the fire under the teakettle and sat down across from her at the table.

"Everything going all right?" he had asked.

Willow had looked up from her French homework in surprise. "What?"

"Everything all right? Cole has been talking to me more than usual lately, asking questions, and you've become . . . not more quiet, exactly, but it's been several days since you asked about your mother."

Willow had allowed her eyes to stray to her homework again.

"Willow?"

She'd sighed and looked up. "I'm not asking questions because I know there aren't any answers."

"About what?"

"About anything to do with Mom. When will she come home? What will happen when she does come home? What will happen if it turns out that she hasn't changed? Will we have to live with her rules again? I know there aren't answers."

Her father had reached across the table and rested his hand on hers. "There might be some answers," he had said. "You will never have to live with the rules again. I promise. I'm not going to let that happen. The moment I see any sign of trouble, I'll take care of it. Things aren't going to be the way they were before."

Willow wanted to believe that. She wanted to believe it more than anything. But she didn't. Not any more than she believed she was a princess in a castle, or that she had traveled back in time to the year the hotel had been built.

She stared out at the pine trees. What had happened to her lovely morning? "I'm not going to let it get ruined," she said aloud. She sat and thought some more, recalling the basket she and Cole and her father had found on their doorstep the day before as they were getting ready to leave on their trip. A secret basket. She had loved the surprise of it, loved that someone had thought of them. Cole had pounced on the chocolate, and her father had smiled a genuine smile as he placed the basket on their hall table.

Willow peered into the corridor. No one was in sight. She stepped into the creaky hallway again, and just like that was propelled back into her morning of discovery. Now she felt a bit like the heroine of an old movie she'd seen recently, *Rebecca*, wandering nervously through the halls of a mansion. She shivered deliciously at the preposterous thought of running into someone as hideous as the creepy Mrs. Danvers.

Willow walked and walked and poked her head through every open door she came across. She found a reading room, stocked with magazines, some of them ancient. She found a room where, apparently, small plays were performed. She found an actual ballroom and for a moment imagined herself twirling around the floor dressed in a gown, looking like Cinderella. And she found a library, which she decided was her favorite room in the entire hotel. It was on the fourth floor and was paneled in dark wood. The carpet was a deep red, and rolling ladders stood by the shelves, which were filled with row after row of books, most bound in leather. Willow let her hand trail along several of them. *Jude the Obscure*, *A Tree Grows in Brooklyn*, *Pride and Prejudice*, *The Wind in the Willows*, *War and Peace*. Willow Hamilton was in heaven.

Willow chose another chair facing out a window, this one with a view of a stand of birch trees, their bare branches scraping the sky, and plopped down into the cushions with a copy of *Rebecca*, which, to her surprise, she had also found. She had seen the movie and now she could read the book. She opened the cover, decided she liked the first sentence very much, but found the story slow going after that. Still, she persevered, curled tightly against the soft fabric of the wing chair, and willed herself not to think about Mrs. Danvers every time she heard a noise in the hallway.

Willow was still plodding through the story when, from a corner of the library, a clock chimed and suddenly she thought to look at her watch. She was supposed to meet Cole and her father in their room in just fifteen minutes in order to have time to dress for Thanksgiving dinner.

What a strange holiday this was, thought Willow. Thanksgiving in a hotel. Her family had never celebrated Thanksgiving anywhere other than in their own dining room. Still, she and Cole had been pleasantly surprised when they'd arrived at Deer Lodge the evening before to learn that the hotel offered a traditional dinner, from turkey to pumpkin pie, to be served at noon the next day.

"We'll have to dress up," their father had said. "No jeans or sneakers in the dining room. And coats and ties for the men."

"I like that," Willow had said. "It's more festive."

Now she left the library, after carefully replacing *Rebecca* in its spot on the shelf, and returned to their suite of rooms. She found her father and Cole already there, in the process of knotting their neckties. When Willow emerged from the bathroom a few minutes later, she was wearing a rippling black skirt, a white blouse, and a red vest.

"Very elegant," commented her father approvingly. "We'll be the best dressed family in the dining room."

Downstairs, Willow watched the other hotel guests as they gathered in the lobby.

"This is exciting!" said Cole suddenly.

Willow could smell turkey and gravy and something sweet, probably the pumpkin pie, and she wanted to share her brother's excitement but found herself instead feeling sorrow.

She missed her mother.

The doors to the dining hall opened then and the guests began to file inside. Willow stood on tiptoe and saw a sea of tables, each covered with a clean, almost sparkling, white cloth, a bowl of gourds and autumn leaves in the center, surrounded by orange candles that glowed softly in the room. It was beautiful, but it wasn't home.

Willow searched the crowd of guests, looking for another family like hers. Why she hoped to find another girl missing her mother, she couldn't have said, and she felt mean, but she continued to look. By now, a waiter had escorted the Hamiltons to their table, and Willow was still scanning the crowd when suddenly Cole pulled at his father's jacket and reached up to whisper something in his ear.

"What was that?" asked Mr. Hamilton.

"That man is alone," said Cole more loudly.

"What man?"

"That one," Cole replied, trying not to point too conspicuously. "We should ask him to sit with us."

Willow looked across the dining room and saw a thin, graying man, several years older than her father, she guessed, who was being shown to a table for one.

"Well, Cole —" Mr. Hamilton began to say.

"Please? Please can't I ask him to come to our table?"

Mr. Hamilton glanced at Willow, who shrugged. Then she looked again at the man sitting motionlessly in the middle of the busy dining room, like a solitary rock in a stream, everything happening around him.

"I think we should invite him," said Willow.

"Oh! I'll do it! I'll do it!" cried Cole, and he dashed away.

When he returned, he was holding the man's hand. "This is Mr. Allen," he said. "I told him we had never had Thanksgiving without our mother before and he said he had never had Thanksgiving without his wife before and that it's nice to eat with a family."

And that was how the Hamiltons met Mr. Allen, who became their good friend and who, years later when Willow got married, gave her a silver bowl that had been given to him and his wife on *their* wedding day and had brought them more happiness than they could have dreamed of.

CHAPTER 12

Thanksgiving Afternoon, November 26th

Olivia Walter sat in the community center, surrounded by her parents, brothers, friends, and neighbors — and her jaw dropped.

Ruby Northrop had just made what even Olivia knew was a terrible mistake. Music was not Olivia's specialty. She lived in a world of science — of facts and theories and principles and properties. She liked music, but she didn't know it or understand it the way Ruby did, and she was confused when the hall became silent and the silence grew and grew like a balloon that threatened to explode. In that impossibly long moment, Olivia turned to her mother, then looked back at the members of the Children's Chorus in time to see Lacey Morris glare at Ruby, and Ruby jump as if she had been poked, which, Olivia suspected, she had been.

At last, Ruby began to sing — alone — but after a line or two, she hesitated and then began to sing again at the same time that a boy began to sing, and now *he* was the one glaring at Ruby.

Uh-oh, thought Olivia.

The song continued, but Ruby's face had turned an alarming shade of red, which didn't fade until well after her second and much longer solo had ended.

Olivia was fascinated. She felt bad for her friend, but she had never seen Ruby make such a mistake. She had seen her cover up other people's mistakes — and onstage, too, right during performances. But this was unprecedented. Ruby had blundered, and her blunder had stood out like a monarch butterfly in a snowstorm.

When the concert ended, Olivia had tried to make her way to Flora and Ruby. What she would have said to Ruby, she wasn't sure. But maybe Ruby would have offered some sort of explanation, and if she had, Olivia would have wanted to hear it. "Mom," Olivia had said urgently, "I have to talk to Ruby for a minute."

"All right, but hurry back. We need to leave for your grandparents'."

"Okay." Olivia had hustled, but she was still two rows away from her friends when she saw Ruby grab Min and pull her toward the exit.

"Ruby!" Olivia had called. "Ruby!"

But Ruby had barged ahead as if she hadn't heard Olivia — and Olivia had used her loudest voice.

"Huh," said Olivia.

She turned back to her own family and quickly forgot about Ruby. Today was Thanksgiving, and Olivia had been looking forward to it ever since her parents had told her and her brothers that this year their family would be spending Thanksgiving with Olivia's mother's parents, her *other* grandparents. Olivia saw Gigi and Poppy, her father's parents, frequently. They lived in Camden Falls, and Needle and Thread was located three doors down from Sincerely Yours. But visits to Paw and Nana, Mrs. Walter's parents, even though they lived just twenty minutes away, were less frequent.

"Who else is going to be at Paw and Nana's?" Olivia had asked, barely able to contain her excitement.

"Let me see. Gigi and Poppy," her mother had said.

"Yay!" Henry had cried.

"And Aunt Stella and Uncle Will."

"Does that mean Ashley will be there?" Olivia had asked, already feeling both shy and excited by the very thought of seeing her sixteen-year-old cousin. Ashley was the kind of sophisticated teenager Olivia aspired to be — and had a good feeling she might never be. Still, it was thrilling to be around her.

"Yes," her mother had replied. "Dawson, too." Dawson was Ashley's brother, who was even older — eighteen — and who always had time for his younger cousins.

"Yippee!" Jack had exclaimed.

And Henry had added, "I wonder if Dawson got his motorcycle yet."

"Lord, I hope not," Olivia's mother had said.

There were to be other cousins and aunts and uncles at Thanksgiving as well, and as the big day had drawn nearer, Olivia had grown more and more excited. With the knowledge that Ashley would be present, she had chosen her outfit for the day with great care. She had, in fact, chosen and discarded no fewer than twenty-six outfits, various combinations of pants and skirts and shirts and sweaters and vests and shoes.

"You girls sure make a big deal out of clothes," Jack had remarked as Olivia had entered the kitchen one evening, wearing yet another ensemble.

Olivia had ignored him. "What about this one?" she had asked her mother.

"I love it!" Mrs. Walter had exclaimed. (She had loved every single one of Olivia's outfits.)

"I thought you only got worked up about outfits for Jaaaaacoooooob," Henry had said. (He'd dragged out the syllables of "Jacob" until the name sounded ridiculously long.)

"Mom!" Olivia had cried. "Why does he bring up Jacob all the time?"

"Because it's fun to tease you about your boyfriend," Henry had said. "That's *boyfriend*. B-O-Y-F-R —"

"Mom!" Olivia had wailed again.

"Ignore, ignore, ignore," Mrs. Walter had whispered in her daughter's ear. "He only teases you because you react. Now, go back upstairs. You look lovely. I think this is the outfit you should wear to Thanksgiving dinner."

Olivia had laid it carefully over the back of her chair and then had changed her mind nine more times.

Now it was Thanksgiving Day and the Children's Chorus concert had ended. Time for Paw and Nana's. Olivia and her family walked back to their house and loaded their van with their contributions to the meal — homemade rolls and glazed carrots and an enormous boxful of Olivia's mother's special chocolates, molded into the shapes of turkeys and oak leaves and pumpkins and even slices of pie.

In the van, which smelled tantalizingly of chocolate and fresh bread, Olivia's emotions seesawed between elation at the thought of seeing Ashley and Dawson and mortification over the outfit she had ultimately decided upon — a crocheted lavender vest over a black shirt, black velvet bell-bottoms, and a purple engineer's cap. Olivia was suddenly certain it was horribly wrong, possibly outlandish. She slumped in her seat. Thanksgiving was ruined before it had even started.

Then her family pulled into Paw and Nana's driveway and Olivia's spirits soared. There were Ashley and Dawson. They were helping Aunt Stella and Uncle

Will unload pans of food from their car, but when they saw the Walters, they set their things down and waved.

"Hey, cousins!" Dawson called cheerfully.

Ashley enveloped Olivia (who had ditched her hat at the last second) in a warm hug as Olivia emerged from the van. Then she held her at arm's length and cried, "Olivia, you look fantastic! When did you get so tall?"

If anyone else had said this to Olivia, she would have shuddered — if for no other reason than because although she *had* grown a bit, she was still the tiniest kid in her entire school. But when Ashley said it, Olivia felt her face grow warm with pleasure.

"I love your outfit," Ashley continued. "Wow. You aren't my little baby cousin anymore."

Olivia beamed. And when Jack piped up, "She has a *boyfriend*," Olivia actually felt grateful to him.

"A boyfriend?! Already?! No way!" said Dawson.

"You have to tell me all about him," Ashley added. And she took Olivia by the elbow and led her inside, saying, "Time for some serious girl talk."

But the girl talk had to wait. The moment Ashley and Olivia entered the house, they were ambushed by relatives. They were gathered in great bearlike hugs and fussed over and admired and kissed. After a particularly scratchy kiss from her mustachioed uncle Ham, Olivia rubbed her cheek and was then put to work in the kitchen, peeling apples for a salad. She had already lost track of her parents and brothers, and couldn't see Ashley, either. In fact, she found it hard to see much of anything around the two buxom aunties who were chopping vegetables across the table.

This is a perfect holiday, thought Olivia as she breathed in the aroma of cloves and sweet potatoes and roasting turkey and melting butter. The kitchen was crowded with bodies, and everyone was talking at top volume. Olivia thought the radio might be playing, too, but it was hard to tell. Outside the window, Olivia could just barely glimpse the blue sky, but even from inside, the air somehow looked cold, and that morning, as she had walked to the community center with her family, she had thought she could smell snow. She hoped for a winter full of blizzards and storms.

"Hey there!"

Someone tapped Olivia on the shoulder and she turned around.

Ashley stood behind her. "I want to hear about Jacob." She turned to Nana. "Olivia's finished," she proclaimed, and tugged her cousin out of the kitchen and into the living room, where they made room for themselves on the end of a sofa. "Okay," said Ashley. "Tell me everything."

Olivia could feel herself blushing, something she wished she had some control over. "Well . . ." She wasn't sure where to begin. "I met him when school started," she said finally. "He's in some of my classes and we're both in the book club at school." Here Olivia hesitated, unsure what Ashley would think of a book club, but her cousin merely nodded encouragingly. "He calls me on the phone a lot," Olivia added.

"Excellent," said Ashley.

"And we . . ." (Olivia knew her blush was deepening) "we went on a date. To a dance at school."

"Girl, no way!"

"Yes. And almost no one else had a date for the dance," Olivia continued, "but Jacob asked me. And later he gave me a birthday card and signed it 'Love, Jacob.'"

"And then they kissed and got married," said a voice from behind the sofa.

Enraged, Olivia jumped to her feet. "Jack!"

But Ashley laid a hand on her arm. "I think he's jealous," she said in a voice just loud enough for Jack to hear. "He wants a girlfriend, but —"

"I do not!" Jack shrieked, and fled from the room.

The front door opened then, ushering in more cousins. After a while, the grown-ups settled themselves in the living room, the younger children were encouraged to run off steam outdoors, and the middle cousins, Olivia included, gathered in the den. All the girls wanted to hear about Jacob, and Olivia told the story of the dance several more times, ignoring the urge to embellish it.

At last the feast was served, and Olivia's large family gathered around three tables, each laden with food. Olivia noted, with immense pleasure, that this was the first year she was not seated at the children's table. She found herself instead among Ashley and Dawson and the other teenagers. To her right, the younger cousins were trying to make Jack laugh hard enough to spray milk out of his nose. To her left, the adults were telling tales from their childhoods. She listened with interest when she heard her mother recall the Thanksgiving dinner — when her mother was a little girl living in their Row House — that had to be postponed because of an autumn blizzard. "Frannie and I were terribly disappointed," she said, and Olivia realized she was talking about Flora and Ruby's mother.

The afternoon spiraled by, darkness falling so that the candles on the dining room table seemed to glow more brightly. The turkey and vegetables and breads were taken away, and just when Olivia thought she was as stuffed as the turkey had been, out came pies and ice cream and the chocolates. Olivia groaned, but she popped one of her mother's chocolate pumpkins in her mouth anyway. The phone rang then, and Paw stood up to answer it.

Nana put her hand on his arm. "Let it be," she said.

"But it might be someone calling to say 'Happy Thanksgiving.'" Paw strode into the kitchen. Moments later, he returned to the dining room and handed the phone to Olivia. "For you," he said.

"I'll bet it's Jacob!" exclaimed Henry.

It took exactly half of one second for Olivia's blush to return. "Hello?" she said. She struggled out of her chair and carried the phone into the bathroom.

"Hi! It's me!" said Jacob. "I just wanted to wish you a happy Thanksgiving."

"Happy Thanksgiving!" Olivia replied. "How did you find me here?"

"I have my ways."

When Olivia returned to the table, she was given a look of pure awe from her ten-year-old cousin Tara, and was clapped on the back by Dawson.

Darkness fell, and one by one the relatives left. As the house quieted, Olivia thought about Jacob. Were they *really* boyfriend and girlfriend? Henry and Jack teased her about having a boyfriend, but she and Jacob never discussed the exact nature of their relationship, although she and Flora and Nikki talked about it. (Olivia suspected that boys didn't concern themselves with such things nearly as often as girls did.)

Was she old enough to have a boyfriend? Did she truly want a boyfriend? She knew she could discuss these questions with Ashley, but the only person she really wanted to call was Flora, and she planned to do just that as soon as she was safely in her bedroom that night.

CHAPTER 13

Thanksgiving Afternoon, November 26th

Several times on the drive from Camden Falls to Three Oaks, Flora snuck a look at Ruby, who was riding sulkily next to her in the backseat of Mr. Pennington's car. Ruby had barely spoken a word since hustling Min out of the community center after the concert. When, on the walk back to Aiken Avenue, Min had said, "So — would you like to talk about what happened this morning?" Ruby had snapped, *"No."* Her mood had not improved when Min had taken Mr. Pennington by the elbow, laughed, and whispered something about drama queens.

The car rolled lazily through the countryside. Flora contemplated the fir trees and imagined them with snow-covered branches sweeping the winter ground. She turned, glanced at her sister, and tried to take her hand, but Ruby jerked it away. "I just wanted to —" Flora began to say.

"Well, don't!" hissed Ruby. She looked quickly at the front seat and added loudly, "And don't anyone say anything about drama queens."

Min made a great show of zipping her lip, and Ruby scowled and stared at her shoes.

When they arrived at Three Oaks, Flora was pleased to find a smiling Mr. Willet waiting in the lobby. He was dressed in a navy suit and a silk tie embroidered with turkeys. Flora was even more pleased when Mr. Willet said that she and Ruby could have the job of bringing Mrs. Willet upstairs to the dining room. "She should be ready and waiting," he added. "I told the nurse on duty that you would be coming for her."

Ruby perked up. "We can go get her ourselves?"

"Yes. Flora, you know what to do, don't you?"

Flora, who had spent more time at Three Oaks than Ruby had, nodded. "When we're on the elevator, I'll be sure to set the brakes on her wheelchair," she said importantly. She took Ruby's hand. "Come on. We have to go down to the lower level." She led her sister along a hall. "Three Oaks is a nice place, don't you think? I wouldn't mind living here."

"Remember when you thought it was depressing?"

"I didn't think Three Oaks was depressing, I thought Mr. Willet's apartment was depressing when it was empty and hadn't been painted yet. Doesn't Mr. Willet seem happy now?"

Ruby considered this. "Yes. He does seem happy."

"Okay. Here's the elevator."

The girls rode down to the lower level, which, because Three Oaks was built on a little hill, was not underground. (Ruby found this confusing.)

Flora led the way down another long hall, past a nurses' station, and stopped when she reached a locked door. She expertly entered a code on a keypad by the door and then pushed the door open. She remembered the first time she had seen the door and the keypad and how she had been horrified by the thought of Mrs. Willet locked into her wing. But she understood why Mrs. Willet and the other people with Alzheimer's couldn't leave their safe quarters. More important, she saw that Mrs. Willet seemed as happy in her new home as Mr. Willet did.

"There she is!" exclaimed Ruby, and she ran across the lobby to a sleepy-eyed Mrs. Willet, who was strapped into her wheelchair.

Mrs. Willet widened her eyes at the sound of Ruby's voice, but her expression remained stony, and Flora had the strange thought that Mrs. Willet looked like a lion, with her proud, sad, motionless face.

Flora approached Mrs. Willet more quietly. "Happy Thanksgiving," she said. She bent to kiss Mrs. Willet's soft, powdery cheek. "You got all dressed up," Flora added, even though she knew that the nurses had dressed her. "Doesn't she look nice?" she said to Ruby, and Ruby nodded. "You're wearing stockings and jewelry and everything, Mrs. Willet. And I think you got your hair done. Did you go to the beauty parlor?"

"Bum-bum-bum-bum," said Mrs. Willet.

Flora caught the eye of a nurse. "Is it okay if I take Mrs. Willet upstairs now?" she asked.

The nurse smiled. "She's all ready to go."

"Can I push her?" Ruby asked, reaching for the handles on the back of the wheelchair.

"Sure. But go slowly. She gets scared if you go too fast. . . . Hey, Mrs. Willet is smiling! Happy Thanksgiving, Mrs. Willet," said Flora again.

"Hi," replied Mrs. Willet, sounding as if she had just woken from a nap.

Ruby tapped Flora's shoulder and whispered, "Does she know who we are?"

Flora shook her head. "I don't think so."

Ruby looked thoughtful. "Okay."

Flora unlocked the door, Ruby pushed the wheelchair through it, and Mrs. Willet said, "Bum-bum-bum-bum-bum" very softly under her breath.

When they reached the lobby upstairs, Min and Mr. Pennington and Mr. Willet were sitting side by side on a couch, leaning toward one another and talking, and Flora thought of the times she had seen them, the three old friends, do just that in Min's living room in the Row House.

Min caught sight of Flora and Ruby and Mrs. Willet and stood up slowly. "There she is!" she said brightly. "Mary Lou, don't you look lovely. Happy Thanksgiving, dear."

"Bum-bum-bum."

"You're in your holiday finest," Mr. Pennington added, and was rewarded with a sudden glowing smile.

"I think she remembers you," Ruby whispered to Mr. Pennington.

"Come look in the dining room," said Mr. Willet to his guests, and he kissed his wife and gently took the wheelchair from Ruby.

When they reached the dining room, Flora peeked inside. She had no idea that at an inn in Maine, just an hour earlier, her friend Willow Hamilton had walked into a dining room that looked almost identical to the one at Three Oaks. "Oh," said Flora. "It's beautiful."

Mr. Willet beamed. "It is nice, isn't it? I wasn't sure what to expect when I moved here, but I've been pleasantly surprised."

"This is elegant," said Min approvingly.

"Nikki's mom is in charge of the dining room," said Flora. "That's her job."

"Which table is ours?" asked Ruby, wide-eyed.

"Follow me," said Mr. Willet, and he led the way to a round table by a picture window. "We're right here."

"Ooh! Chocolate turkeys!" exclaimed Ruby, sizing up the decorations.

"I bought those specially," said Mr. Willet. "They came from Sincerely Yours."

"Min? Could I go find Mrs. Sherman?" asked Flora. "Ruby and I want to wish her a happy Thanksgiving."

Min granted permission, and Flora and Ruby

walked around the bustling dining room until they caught sight of Nikki's mother giving instructions to a group of waiters. They waved discreetly to her and called, "Happy Thanksgiving!"

She smiled and waved back.

"She's busy," said Flora. "This is a busy place. Actually, I'm glad there's so much going on. It takes my mind off of —"

"Don't say it!" cried Ruby. "Can people not talk about *any*thing except my one teensy mistake?"

"I was going to say that it takes my mind off of Aunt Allie and the baby."

"Oh," said Ruby.

"Aren't you afraid of what I'm afraid of?"

"What are you afraid of?"

"I'm afraid the birth parents will change their minds. Aren't you?"

"I'm more afraid the baby will be a girl. I just *have* to have a boy cousin. Anyway, don't the birth parents have a right to change their minds? It's their baby."

"I know, I know," said Flora. "But Aunt Allie wants a baby so badly and . . . oh, why is everything always so complicated?"

"Because you're twelve," Ruby replied grouchily.

"You'd better get rid of that attitude before we go back to the table," said Flora.

"All I have to do is think about chocolate turkeys," said Ruby airily. "*Mmmm.* Chocolate. Yum. See? My good mood is back."

Flora and Ruby returned to the table and took their seats. Flora politely put her napkin in her lap. She saw that Min had taken Mrs. Willet's hand and was saying earnestly to her, "Do you remember the apple tree in the Jensens' front yard? Well, not two weeks ago it was hit by lightning and it split right in two."

Mrs. Willet stared at Min in a concentrated manner.

Mr. Pennington pulled his wallet out of his pocket and showed Mr. Willet some photos.

A waiter approached the table with a tray of small bowls, which turned out to hold corn chowder.

Ruby eyed the chocolate turkeys fondly.

"I love Thanksgiving!" said Flora suddenly, and everyone smiled at her.

"Min? Any news from Allie?" Mr. Willet asked when the waiter had left.

"She called this morning before the concert" (at the mention of the concert, Ruby glared ferociously into her soup) "but only to say that nothing has happened."

At that very moment, Min's cell phone rang.

"Min!" exclaimed Flora, horrified. Min rarely used her cell phone, and she had certainly never left it on during a meal in a fancy dining room. Min said people who took phone calls at the table were as uncivilized as hyenas.

"I have to leave it on in case Allie calls," said Min hurriedly.

"Maybe the baby's here!" shrieked Ruby. "Aunt Allie wouldn't call us during dinner unless it was really important!"

"Hush, Ruby," said Min. She held the phone to her ear, ducked her head, and said quietly, "Hello? . . . Well, my goodness!" she exclaimed after a pause. "Happy Thanksgiving to you, too! It's so nice to hear your voice."

"I guess it isn't Aunt Allie," said Ruby.

Min kept the conversation brief, clicked off the phone, and said, "That was my old friend Sadie. I haven't spoken to her in ages. I'll have to call her back tonight."

When the soup bowls were empty, the waiter collected them and passed around plates of salad.

Min's phone rang again.

"He's here! My new cousin is here!" yelped Ruby.

"*He's* here?" said Flora.

"I just know it's a boy."

Min was speaking quietly into the phone. "No. No news yet," Flora heard her say.

Ruby shook her head sadly. "Not Aunt Allie. Hey, we should start fining Min for taking calls during a meal."

Min cleared her throat as she put the phone back in her purse. "That was Gigi, wondering if we'd heard anything," she murmured.

The salad plates were removed, and a few minutes later, the waiter returned with his tray piled high with covered dishes.

"This is it," said Ruby. "Turkey time."

As each plate was set down, the waiter lifted the cover to reveal turkey with cranberry sauce and gravy, stuffing, mashed potatoes, peas, and squash.

"This is heaven," said Min. "Simply heaven."

"Who would like to say the blessing?" asked Mr. Willet. "Flora?"

Flora was so surprised by the request that she forgot to feel shy. She bowed her head and said, "Thank you for this holiday. I'm glad we can all be together and that we can celebrate with the Willets. Thank you for the food. And thank you for our new cousin. Happy Thanksgiving."

"Lovely," said Mr. Willet.

Min's phone didn't ring again until just before a dessert of apple pie with whipped cream was served. "That was Paula Edwards," said Min apologetically. "Wanted to know if the baby was here yet." She laid the phone on the table.

In a flash, Mrs. Willet picked up the phone and began to examine it, tentatively pressing buttons and finally shaking it.

"Um, Min?" said Flora urgently. "Look."

Everyone looked at Mrs. Willet. Min reached for the phone and tried to pry it from her fingers, but Mrs. Willet wouldn't let go.

Mr. Willet held out his hand. "Could I have that for just a moment, Mary Lou?" he asked.

Mrs. Willet pressed another button.

"Mary Lou?" he said again.

Mrs. Willet dropped the phone, which narrowly missed landing in a glass of water, and Min grabbed it and slipped it into her purse.

Flora glanced at Ruby. Ruby was looking at Flora. Flora bit the insides of her cheeks, then pretended to search busily for something under the table. Mrs. Willet and the phone shouldn't have been funny at all, but Flora was inches away from exploding into laughter.

Ruby bent down, too, and Flora hissed, "Sit up! If I look at you now I'll never stop laughing."

Ruby sat up, Flora gained control of herself, and soon dinner was over and everyone was pushing their chairs away from the table. They walked slowly out of the dining room, Min holding her stomach and saying, "I'm stuffed!"

They chatted in the lobby until Mr. Willet said, "Mary Lou is falling asleep. I'd better take her downstairs. I'll be back in just a few minutes."

"I'll come with you," said Flora.

Along the hall to the elevator, down to the lower level, along another hall, and they reached the locked door. Flora pressed buttons and the door opened. Mr. Willet wheeled the chair through and stopped it by the nurses' station.

"Hey, Mrs. Willet is awake again," announced Flora.

Mr. Willet peered around to look at his wife. She smiled at him.

"Okay, honey, I have to go now," he said briskly. "I need to say good-bye to our guests. I'll see you tomorrow." He kissed her on the forehead and strode back to the door.

"Good-bye, Mrs. Willet," said Flora. "Happy Thanksgiving." She followed Mr. Willet out the door, and as it locked behind her, she turned and glanced through the window. "Mr. Willet!" she exclaimed in alarm. "Mrs. Willet's crying."

Mrs. Willet was sitting motionless in her chair, but her face had crumpled in the way that Alyssa Morris's did when she was about to burst into tears. The corners of her mouth were turned down, her lower lip was poking out, and she was squinting her eyes.

"It's okay," Mr. Willet said gently to Flora. "Just wait a bit."

A nurse wheeled Mrs. Willet away, and when Flora peeked through the window again, she saw Mrs. Willet seated contentedly in front of a television, a smile on her face.

"She's already forgotten we left," said Mr. Willet. "She's probably even forgotten that she was sad. That's just the way it is."

In the car on the way home, Flora tried not to remember Mrs. Willet's face as she had watched her husband leave. She thought instead of the fancy dining room and the chocolate turkeys and Mrs. Sherman efficiently in charge of the dinner. She was staring lazily out the window into the last light of the day when Min's phone rang once again.

"Hello?" said Min. "Allie?"

Flora felt her stomach jump.

"It was? When? What is it?"

There was a long silence during which Ruby grabbed Flora's hand and they clung to each other. Flora didn't even try to make out the rest of Min's side of the conversation. She waited until Min had clicked off the phone and then she shrieked, "Tell us!"

"The baby's here!" exclaimed Min. "It's a girl."

"Yes!" cried Flora. "Yes, yes, yes! A girl! A girl cousin! A girl to baby-sit for. A girl to sew for!"

"A darn *girl*?" squawked Ruby. "But you can't name a girl Douglas."

Mr. Pennington let out a guffaw. Then he turned to Min. "Is the baby okay? She's pretty early."

"She's tiny, and she and the mother are both experiencing a few problems, but the doctors expect them to be fine. The baby will probably have to stay in the hospital for two more weeks, though. Allie won't be bringing her home this weekend."

Ruby drew in her breath. "We're still going to New York tomorrow, aren't we?"

Flora elbowed her sister, but Ruby elbowed her right back.

"Yes, we're still going," said Min, and her cell phone screeched from her purse. "Goodness me, what now?" she muttered.

It was Allie calling back. "She wants me to put her on speakerphone," said Min. She pressed a button. "Go ahead, Allie."

Allie's voice filled the car. "I forgot to tell you the most important thing." She paused. "I decided what to name the baby."

"Probably not Douglas," murmured Flora.

"I have decided," Allie continued, "to name her Jane Marie. Janie for short."

"Our middle names!" exclaimed Flora.

"Mine comes first," noted Ruby.

"Allie, what a lovely idea," said Min.

I have a namesake, thought Flora as the car turned onto Aiken Avenue later. A cousin and a namesake all at once.

CHAPTER 14

Thanksgiving Evening, November 26ᵗʰ

Hilary Nelson hadn't said much about it (she didn't want to hurt her parents' feelings), but she had not been looking forward to Thanksgiving. After all her family had been through that year — moving to Camden Falls, losing their home in a fire, starting a business at a time when money was tight and the Nelsons had been warned against a new venture — she felt that the very least she could expect was a cozy holiday at home. She wanted to wake up to the smell of turkey roasting in the oven and go to Ruby's concert with her parents and her brother. She wanted to help her mother set the table with their good china and eat a big meal in the middle of the afternoon and later, at what should be dinnertime, help herself to two different kinds of pie. She wanted to spend the day at home with her family.

But the Nelsons were now the owners of the Marquis Diner, so Hilary had been chagrined, although not necessarily surprised, when her parents had announced that the diner would be open for business on Thanksgiving Day.

"But what about *our* Thanksgiving?" Hilary had wailed.

"We'll close the diner at six and have our own dinner in the evening," her father had replied.

"What are we going to have? Reuben sandwiches and coleslaw?"

Her mother had eyed her. "I'll make our food ahead of time. We'll have a real turkey dinner, just like we always do. And just like we'll offer in the diner," she'd added. "Do you really think we're not going to serve a turkey dinner on Thanksgiving?"

"This is going to be one of our biggest days ever," her father had added. "We can't afford not to be open. This has been a rough enough year already."

"I know," Hilary had said. "Sorry."

Hilary had made no further comments about their Thanksgiving plans, but still, whenever she thought about the holiday, she felt a little pang in her stomach. So many things were no longer the way they used to be.

When Hilary awoke on Thanksgiving morning, she found that the pang was no longer little. It was quite large, and Hilary had a good cry in her bedroom before she padded down the hallway to the kitchen. She had no idea that by evening the pang would have disappeared entirely, replaced with excitement and a number of unexpected occurrences.

Hilary stood at the front window of their apartment, a piece of toast in one hand, a glass of orange juice in the other. Below her, Main Street was coming to life. Most of the stores and businesses were closed, of course. ("But *we'll* be open," Hilary mumbled sourly.) Still, there was Mr. Pennington taking Jacques for an early morning walk, and Mrs. Edwards buying a paper at the newsstand, and several cars driving lazily through town.

Thirteen and a half hours later, with the day behind her, Hilary (in a much brighter mood) was at the window again. Now the stores on Main Street glowed pleasantly beneath the streetlights. Most of their windows were dark, but the town was busy. People who had eaten their holiday meal at Fig Tree streamed happily out the door and made their way to their cars. Hilary craned her neck as far to the right as possible and noted that Frank had opened Frank's Beans for the evening. People were sitting on the stools at the window, holding cups of Autumn Celebration tea and Pumpkin Spice latte.

Hilary's stomach was pleasantly full of turkey and stuffing and pie, and her head was full of the events of the day. When the phone rang and her father called,

"Hilary, for you! It's Ruby!" she leaped to her feet and grabbed the receiver. Then she settled by the window again. "Ruby!" she exclaimed. "You won't believe everything that happened today."

"You won't believe my news, either!" cried Ruby. "And I get to tell it first because whatever your news is, I promise mine's more exciting. Plus, I called you."

Hilary had been about to launch into the details of her day, but she said, "Okay. You go first."

"All right. My news is . . ." Ruby paused like an announcer on a game show.

"What? What?" said Hilary.

"My news is . . . that the baby was born."

"Yes!" shrieked Hilary. "What is it?"

"Well, it's a girl. But that's okay because her name is Jane Marie. Get it? Jane is my middle name, and Marie is Flora's middle name. And the baby is going to be called Janie, after me."

"That's great!" said Hilary. "When will she come home?"

"Not for a while. A couple of weeks or so. But she'll be here for Christmas."

"Oh. A baby for Christmas," said Hilary with a sigh. "That's going to be so much fun."

"What's your news?" asked Ruby.

"There are a whole bunch of things," Hilary replied, and she thought back to that morning when she and Spencer had at last left the apartment and gone downstairs to the diner. Their parents had given them permission to watch part of the Thanksgiving parade on TV before they began their work.

"We'll get things set up," their mother had said. "You can join us any time before noon."

By the time they'd entered the diner, they'd found each table set with a pair of paper Pilgrims and a tiny vase containing a russet-colored chrysanthemum. On the chalkboard by the front door was a description of the day's special turkey dinner, which Mrs. Nelson had written in jaunty red and yellow and orange. Pamela, the young waitress who had just started working at the Marquis, had added a brilliant border of vines and pumpkins to the chalkboard. Despite herself, Hilary had begun to feel rather festive. She'd felt even better when her mother had pinned a yellow rose to her shirt. "Dad bought us corsages," she told Ruby.

"So, who ate in the diner today?" Ruby wanted to know.

"A whole bunch of people I wouldn't have expected," Hilary replied, although she wasn't at all sure whom she *had* expected.

"Oh." Ruby sounded disappointed. "Was it just a bunch of people who didn't have anywhere else to go? Lonely people eating by themselves?"

"*No,*" said Hilary somewhat huffily.

She thought of how quiet the diner had been when it opened at noon. At 12:15, when no customers had arrived, she had looked anxiously at her watch. This wasn't the Thanksgiving she had hoped for, but she knew her parents were counting on a certain amount of business, and she didn't want them to be disappointed.

"Dad," Hilary had said urgently. Her father was standing across the diner, readying things behind the counter. Hilary pointed dramatically at the Coca-Cola clock on the wall. "It's twelve-fif*teen*," she'd said.

"Don't worry," her father had replied.

At twelve-twenty, their first customers arrived, and Hilary's mouth fell open.

"Who was it?" Ruby asked breathlessly.

"It was . . ." Hilary paused even longer than Ruby had paused when she had given Hilary the baby news. "It was . . . Mrs. Caldwell. And her family."

"Our *teacher*? What was she doing there?"

"That's just what I asked her."

Hilary told Ruby about the sheepish look on Mrs. Caldwell's face as she'd entered the Marquis, followed by a man and two small boys.

"You got to see her *husband*?!" exclaimed Ruby.

"Yup. And her two sons."

"*She* gets *boys*."

"I was so surprised that I said, 'Mrs. Caldwell! You didn't tell me you were going to eat here today.'"

Mrs. Caldwell had smiled ruefully at Hilary. "We had a tiny accident at home."

"Our oven caught fire!" announced one of the boys.

"We put the fire out, but we won't be able to use the oven until the repairman has taken a look at it," added Mrs. Caldwell.

"The firefighters came!" announced the other boy. "It was really cool. You should see our kitchen. Water everywhere."

"The turkey's dripping wet," said the first boy. "It got sprayed with a hose."

"It almost exploded."

Hilary, feeling highly self-conscious, had said, "May I show you to a table? You're our first customers of the day. You can sit anywhere you want."

The Caldwells chose a table by the window, and Hilary brought them their menus and filled their glasses with water. "You can order anything from the regular menu," she said, "or you can have the special turkey dinner."

"Turkey dinner!" exclaimed the boys in unison.

"Ditto," said Mr. and Mrs. Caldwell.

"So," Hilary said to Ruby, "guess who came in next."

"Do I really have to guess? I'll probably get it wrong."

"Okay. I'll tell you. Mrs. Grindle."

"Oh, EW!" cried Ruby. "Why can't she stay at home and be crabby there? Why does she have to go out in public and ruin other people's holidays?"

"Well, she wasn't that bad," replied Hilary. "Actually, I felt a little sorry for her."

Mrs. Grindle had poked her head through the door and looked around the nearly empty diner for a few moments before apparently deciding to stay. Hilary had left the Caldwells and bustled across the room to show Mrs. Grindle to another one of the window tables.

"She ordered the turkey dinner, too," Hilary reported. "And then she just sat and ate by herself."

"Did anybody *not* order the turkey dinner today?" asked Ruby.

"A few people. And one of them was — you won't believe this."

"Who? Who?"

"Okay. You know Miss Drew?"

"The second-grade teacher?"

"Yup."

"She's Mae Sherman's teacher this year. She came to the diner? And she didn't eat turkey?"

"She came to the diner, all right, but she had turkey. It was the person she was with who ordered spaghetti."

"Spaghetti! Who eats spaghetti on Thanksgiving?"

"Miss Drew's . . . boyfriend."

Ruby let forth with a shriek. "Miss Drew has a boyfriend?! Wait until I tell Mae. What does he look like? Is he nice?"

Hilary filled Ruby in on the rest of the day's events, although nothing quite lived up to the boyfriend news. "So," she finally said, "how was the concert? You didn't tell me."

"Oh . . ." Ruby considered lying, but knew she would be caught eventually, so she settled on replying, "It was all right. You know how those things are."

Hilary had no idea how the concerts were since she hadn't been to one yet, but all she said was, "Tell me about your trip tomorrow."

So Ruby did, and as Hilary listened to the details of the train ride and the sights Ruby was sure to see, she decided that this had been the most interesting Thanksgiving of her life.

CHAPTER 15

Friday Morning, November 27th

Ruby awoke in a great big hurry the next morning. Images of New York and the trip were flashing through her brain as swiftly as the train she would soon be riding. She thought of the Christmas show at Radio City Music Hall. Ruby had seen ads for it since the end of September and had begged Min to get tickets, but none were available. It was sold out. Min had been able, however, to get tickets to a new musical called *Spotlight*, and Ruby was thrilled with this turn of events. She had heard the music from *Spotlight*, even though the show didn't have any roles for children in it. Ordinarily, Ruby was interested only in shows in which she might play a part: *The Wizard of Oz*, *The Sound of Music*, *Annie*. But she very much liked the music from *Spotlight*, especially the song about the tap dancer.

Ruby lay in her bed, humming and thinking. The show would be the highlight of the trip, of course. But then there were the restaurants. Ruby hoped to sample some exotic food. Italian, maybe, or French. Perhaps she could try snails, although she had a strong sense that she wouldn't like them. She had once heard someone describe them as buttered rubber, which was highly unappealing.

"Shopping," said Ruby out loud, counting off activities on her fingers as she lay in her bed. "Statue of Liberty. Empire State Building. Central Park."

The phone rang.

Ruby leaped out of bed, sprang across her room, and flung open her door just in time to hear Min, who was standing in the front hall at the bottom of the stairs, say, "Ms. Angelo? Yes, this is Mindy Read."

Ruby stopped short. This couldn't be good. She took a step forward, then, glad she was barefoot, stood silently, and listened. There wasn't much to hear, mostly a lot of dead air on Min's end. The choral director was doing all the talking. A very bad sign.

At last, Ruby heard Min say, "Yes, of course I'll speak with her. I agree wholeheartedly. . . . It *is* a problem. It's been a problem in school, too." (Inwardly, Ruby groaned.) A few moments later, Min said, "For how long? . . . Several months? What about the Christmas concert? . . . Well, I know she'll be disappointed, but I understand your decision."

At these words, Ruby felt herself grow cold. Not shivery cold, but nervous cold. She considered creeping back into her bed but recalled that she had promised Min she would be up at eight that morning and ready to leave for the train station by nine. This was not the time to appear lazy. She had a feeling that a talk about responsibility was at hand.

Ruby decided to pretend nothing was wrong. She gathered herself together and trotted down the stairs. "Good morning!" she chirped. "It's eight-oh-five and I'm out of bed, just like I promised. See how I can keep my — Min, is something wrong?"

Min eyed Ruby darkly. "That was Ms. Angelo on the phone."

"Lovely Ms. Angelo," said Ruby. "She's the best choral director I've ever worked with." (She was only the second choral director Ruby had worked with.)

"I'm glad you think so. Do you trust her judgment, Ruby?"

"Um . . ."

"Because Ms. Angelo had a few things to say about your performance yesterday."

"She did?"

"As you can imagine, she was disappointed."

Ruby slumped into an armchair. "How disappointed?"

"Very."

"Am I in trouble?"

"You're on probation."

"What does that mean?"

"Well, in this case, it means that Ms. Angelo is going to be watching you carefully over the next few months. She's going to pay close attention to you during rehearsals. If she's satisfied with what she sees, then you may remain in the chorus. But if your attitude doesn't improve, she will ask you to leave. Also, until she makes her decision, you will not be singing any solos."

"But I have the main solo in the Christmas concert!" cried Ruby. "Min, this isn't fair! Just because I made one little mistake." She paused. "And what's wrong with my attitude?"

"Ruby, it wasn't a little mistake. It was a big one. But more important, you wouldn't have made it if you had attended rehearsals and had done all your practicing. And that's what's wrong with your attitude. You've become a bit . . . cocky. We've had this talk before, where your schoolwork is concerned."

"I only missed one rehearsal! One teeny rehearsal."

"No, you missed two. And the second one was the last rehearsal before the concert. You could have attended it, but you decided you were tired and that you knew your part anyway. I think you felt that you didn't really need to go to the rehearsal."

"But, Min, everyone makes mistakes. You say that yourself all the time."

"That's true. But it's one thing to make a mistake when you're trying your hardest —"

"I was trying my hardest!"

"I don't think so, honey. If you were trying your hardest, you would have gone to the rehearsal."

Ruby let out an exasperated sigh. "I wasn't the only one making mistakes. Germaine was saying 'No Peeking' instead of 'Topeka.' And the altos were flat."

"Ruby, I'm not going to argue with you. You haven't been taking chorus seriously this fall, you haven't been practicing at home, and you made a huge mistake during the recital yesterday. Ms. Angelo has every right to put you on probation."

"But what about my Christmas solo?" Ruby wailed.

"I don't know. I suppose someone else will sing it."

"Lacey," said Ruby venomously. "Lacey will get the solo."

"Well, I hope she works hard on it."

"She will." Ruby slumped in the chair until she could slump no farther.

Min looked at her seriously for several moments. "You have told me many times that you want to become a professional performer one day."

"Yes!" exclaimed Ruby. "I do."

"Then you need to start acting like a professional." Min heaved herself up from the couch. She looked at her watch. "Come have breakfast now, Ruby. We should leave in forty-five minutes. Are you all packed?"

"Yes," said Ruby, who would have said yes even if she weren't packed.

"Good. I defrosted some sticky buns this morning. And I'll make scrambled eggs."

"Fine." Ruby slid sulkily into her seat at the table.

Flora was already in the kitchen, eating a bun and consulting a list. "Min," she said, "this is my packing list. Everything on it is in my suitcase." She handed the list to her grandmother. "Do you think I've forgotten anything?"

"Show-off," muttered Ruby.

"What?" said Flora.

"Nothing."

Min eyed Ruby. "I hope it was nothing." She took the list from Flora. "This looks fine, honey. I'm glad you remembered something nice for tomorrow night."

Ruby, reaching for a glass of juice, paused, hand in midair. Something nice for tomorrow night. For . . . ? Oh, for the theatre. Min had told her and Flora to make sure to pack one fancy outfit, and Ruby had forgotten. She finished her juice, took three bites of a sticky bun, told Min she was too excited to eat eggs, and ran to her bedroom, where she pulled a dress out of her closet and stuffed it into her suitcase. She was about to zip the suitcase closed when she realized that unless she wanted to wear the dress with sneakers she would also need to pack her good shoes. She was just stuffing them in as well when Min called up the stairs, "Ready, Ruby?"

"Yup!" said Ruby, who now was not at all sure she was ready. What else had Min told her and Flora to pack? She pawed frantically through her suitcase. Pajamas, underwear, hairbrush . . . she was already wearing jeans (the good pair with no holes in the knees) and her sneakers. Money! She must remember to bring along her money so she could buy her friends very cool Christmas gifts from New York City. Her friends, she thought, no longer included Lacey. She planned to buy Lacey a big fat nothing for Christmas.

Ruby took one last look in her suitcase, threw in an additional T-shirt, just in case, and then two of her china animals, which she wrapped in a pair of socks, and zipped the case shut.

"There," she said.

She lugged the suitcase down the stairs. Min and Flora were waiting in the front hall with their suitcases.

"Oh, no," Ruby moaned suddenly. "Now we have to say good-bye to King Comma and Daisy Dear. King has never stayed by himself here in the Row Houses."

"Yes, he has," said Flora.

Ruby shook her head. "No, he hasn't. Not overnight."

"King and Daisy will be in Rudy Pennington's good hands," said Min.

"Yeah," said Flora. "They love him. They'll be fine."

"I guess." Ruby swept King Comma into her arms and kissed the top of his head. "You behave," she told him. "Be nice to Mr. Pennington. And no scaring Daisy, okay?" King Comma had taken to hiding under Ruby's bed and darting out at Daisy as she walked by, which always made Daisy jump and then look at Ruby or Flora or Min with great wounded eyes.

"All right. Let's get a move on," said Min. "Our train leaves in forty-five minutes."

Ruby tried hard to enjoy the start of her vacation, but visions of Ms. Angelo and Lacey — Lacey angelically singing the Christmas solo — kept creeping into her mind. As Min drove slowly along Aiken Avenue and their car passed the Morrises' house, Ruby rolled down her window and stuck her fist outside.

"What are you doing?" asked Flora.

Ruby hastily withdrew her hand. "Nothing."

Min glanced at Ruby in the rearview mirror. "It sort of looked like you were giving someone the thumbs-down sign. I'd hate to think that was true."

Ruby said nothing.

Min turned a corner and then another corner and steered the car along Main Street.

"Look!" cried Flora. "There's Mr. Freedly. He's putting up the Christmas decorations. Can you believe a whole year has gone by since we saw him do that the first time?"

Now Ruby did manage to forget about Ms. Angelo and the chorus. She gazed at Main Street as it began its annual transformation. "The decorations are different this year," she remarked. "Mr. Freedly is putting bells on every lamppost."

"The bells will light up at night," said Min.

"And everyone is decorating the store windows," added Flora. She turned to her sister. "Just wait until we get to New York. Think what the decorations will look like there."

"They'll be beautiful," said Ruby dreamily.

And then Min spoiled everything by driving by the community center. In a flash, Ruby was back on the risers, standing mutely before an expectant audience; just standing there when she should have begun her solo. When at last she had opened her mouth, everyone had stared at her, and not in a good way.

Ruby crossed her arms and looked bleakly at the passing countryside. She could think of nothing that would cheer her, not even baby Janie.

CHAPTER 16

Friday, November 27ᵗʰ

When Min parked the car at the train station, Flora took a look at Ruby's glowering face and made a decision. She waited until Min was talking to the ticket agent and then she pulled Ruby aside and whispered loudly, "Ruby, don't you dare spoil this vacation. You were the one who wanted to go to New York so badly, and Min planned the trip and took time off from the store and got tickets to a show and everything. So *do not* pout. Because if you start, I'm going to tell Min that she might as well cut the trip short and take us back home right away. I swear I will do that." Before Ruby could say anything, Flora continued, "Okay. Here comes Min with the tickets. Now, smile and be pleasant. And *mean* it."

Ruby looked stunned by what her sister had said, and Flora felt a bit stunned. But she wasn't going to take any of it back.

"Okay, girls," said Min. "Track three. The train will be here in ten minutes."

"Do you think we could get something to eat in the club car?" Flora asked. "That would be so much fun."

"Certainly," said Min.

"What's a club car?" asked Ruby.

"It's kind of like a snack bar on wheels."

Flora watched her sister's face brighten. "Cool!" exclaimed Ruby, and Flora relaxed.

The train rolled past hills and mountains. It sped by cities and towns. Flora and Min sat in a seat facing Ruby; Flora and Ruby were glued to the windows. When their stomachs began to grumble, the girls were allowed to go to the club car by themselves and buy snacks. They returned to the seats with chips and soda and a cup of tea for Min.

Flora was the first to see skyscrapers in the distance.

"There it is!" cried Flora. "New York!"

"The Big Apple!" exclaimed Ruby, twisting around in her seat.

"I think I see the Empire State Building!" said Flora. She was slightly disappointed when, seconds later, the train sped into a tunnel and the view of the city disappeared, but she gazed out the darkened windows anyway.

"Here we are," said Min presently as the train drew to a stop. "Grand Central."

Flora and Ruby and Min collected their suitcases, stepped onto the platform, and walked into an enormous room with a gloriously painted ceiling. "*This* is a train station?" said Flora.

On the ceiling, in gold against a brilliant blue background, were thousands of stars. "The constellations," whispered Flora.

Ruby dropped her suitcase as she tipped her head back and stared. She stared for so long that she nearly lost her balance. Flora caught her elbow. "Wow," said Ruby.

Outside, Min told the girls that they were going to walk for several blocks. And so they did, until suddenly Min hopped off the curb and stuck out her hand, and to Flora's amazement, a cab swerved out of the traffic and came to a stop in front of them. The driver popped open the trunk and stepped onto the sidewalk to load the suitcases inside. Min slid into the backseat of the cab, and a very surprised Flora and Ruby slid in after her.

"Min! How did you know how to do that?" asked Flora.

"Hail a cab? I have my ways," she replied.

The driver closed his door and turned to look at Min, who said, "Twelfth Street between Fifth and Sixth, please."

The cab sped off.

Once again, Flora was glued to the window. "I've never *seen* so many people," she said. "And everyone is moving so *fast*."

"Just like on TV," added Ruby.

Flora marveled at the bustle and activity. There was movement everywhere. People hurried down sidewalks and darted across streets. Cars and trucks and buses and cabs screeched around corners. A man rode by on his bicycle, a small dog running beside him on his leash. A woman zoomed along on her scooter. Doors opened and closed. A little boy jumped up and down, screeching, "But I *want* a doughnut! I *want* one!"

"In just this one block," said Flora when the cab was stuck in traffic, "I see three restaurants, a shoe store, a store called Funny Cry Happy —"

"Funny Cry Happy? What do you think they sell in *there*?" asked Ruby.

"A pizza place," Flora continued, craning her neck to the left, "a Starbucks, a little grocery store, and a dry cleaner."

"Welcome to New York," said Min.

At last, the cab turned onto a quiet tree-lined street, and Min leaned forward and said to the driver, "It's the big building on the left."

The cab pulled up to the sidewalk, the trunk was popped open again, and Flora and Ruby and Min climbed out and claimed their suitcases. Min paid the driver, and Flora gawked at the fountain in front of the building and the doorman in his fancy uniform who was standing at the entrance.

"Follow me, girls," said Min, and she strode toward the doorman. "Good morning," she greeted him. "We're here to visit Allie Read, who's staying in 3E."

The doorman smiled at them and led them inside to a small desk. He picked up a phone and as he was dialing it he said to Min, "May I have your name, please?"

"Mindy Read," she replied. "I'm Allie's mother."

The doorman spoke into the phone, then hung it up and said, "Go on up. The elevator's over there on the right."

"Oh, Min, this is so exciting!" said Flora in a hushed voice as they stepped into the elevator. "*Every*thing is so exciting. Imagine us in a New York City apartment building. I feel like I'm in a movie."

The elevator rose to the third floor, and when the door opened, Allie was waiting for them. "I can't believe you're here!" she said, and then burst into tears and clung to Min. "Sorry," she said a few moments later. "Sorry. I'm so . . . emotional. You'd think *I* was the one who just gave birth."

"What's the news?" asked Min as Allie led them down a hallway. "Anything since last night?"

Allie shook her head. "No. And I don't think I'll get to see the baby for a while. Probably not until she's ready to come home with me. Even then I won't meet the birth parents. Everything will be handled through lawyers. But as far as I know, nothing has changed, and Janie and her mom are doing as well as the doctors could hope." Allie opened a door marked 3E. "Here we are," she said.

Flora stepped into a foyer with four doorways leading to other rooms, and a small hall leading to more rooms in the back. "This is big!" she exclaimed. "I thought an apartment would be small." She poked her head into a kitchen, a living room, a dining room, an office, and two bedrooms. "Wow!" she said. "Wow!"

"I could live here," said Ruby, setting down her suitcase.

"Hey, look out this window," said Flora. "You can see right into those apartments across the street. Boy, you don't really have much privacy in an apartment."

"Well, who cares?" replied Ruby. "It's New York, *hello*. Hey, Aunt Allie, do you think any movie stars live in those apartments? Just think, Flora, we could be looking right into Julie Andrews's apartment. Or Meryl Streep's. Ooh, ooh! Or George Clooney's! Wouldn't that be cool?"

"Somehow I think their apartments are fancier than the ones you're looking into," said Aunt Allie. "Here, let me show you where you're going to sleep. You can unpack a bit, and then we'll go out for lunch. How would you like to eat in a French bistro?"

"Ohhhh," breathed Flora. "A French bistro."

"Just like on *I Love Lucy* when Lucy orders the snails," said Ruby. "Hey! Now's my chance to try snails."

"You're really going to order snails?" asked Flora incredulously.

"Yup," said Ruby. "I'm definitely going to think about possibly ordering snails."

Flora decided the bistro was the most exotic place she had ever been in, even though the waiters and waitresses didn't speak French, as she had hoped they would. Still, she and Ruby and Min and Aunt Allie were shown to a small round table with fancy little chairs and given menus featuring dishes with names like *croque monsieur* and *steak au poivre*.

"Look, Ruby," said Aunt Allie. "Here are your snails. See where it says *escargots*?"

Ruby turned slightly pale. "So they really are on the menu," she murmured. "Well," she said after a few moments, "if I ordered them, would you all try one?"

"No way," said Flora.

"No, thank you," said Min.

"You're on your own," said Allie.

Ruby continued to study the menu. "Do you think they have grilled cheese sandwiches?" she finally asked. Flora snorted. "Well, what are *you* going to have?" Ruby wanted to know.

"A hamburger and French fries. At least the fries are French."

After lunch, Aunt Allie, Min, Flora, and Ruby took the subway uptown. Flora was fascinated. "Riding in an underground train," she marveled. "Just imagine what's above us. Buses, stores, apartment buildings, skyscrapers. . . . How come the subway tunnels don't collapse under those tons and tons of weight?"

"Let's not think about that," said Min faintly.

When they stepped out of the subway, Allie said, "What shall we do first? Go to Central Park? Walk down Fifth Avenue?"

"Fifth Avenue," said Flora.

"Central Park," said Ruby.

Allie tossed a coin in the air and Ruby won. They strolled through Central Park and Flora couldn't believe they were right in the middle of a huge city. "It feels almost like the country here," she said.

"Except for those people on bicycles and skateboards and scooters. And that woman over there drumming. And those guys break-dancing," said Ruby.

"Well, you know what I mean," said Flora. "I can barely see any buildings from here."

They turned around and walked back to Fifth Avenue. They poked their heads into jewelry stores. In one, Flora saw a diamond-and-emerald necklace priced at $27,000. "Ruby!" she exclaimed in a whisper. "Look at this! At first I thought it cost twenty-seven dollars, and then I realized it's twenty-seven *thousand* dollars. Who spends that much money on a necklace?"

Ruby sucked in her breath. "A billionaire, I guess. But I'll bet no one will buy it. I'll bet if we came back in five years, it would still be here."

"Aunt Allie?" said Flora as they left the jewelry store. "Is there any place where I can buy presents for my friends? I mean, presents I can afford? I want to get souvenirs and Christmas presents."

"Me, too," said Ruby.

They walked until they found a gift shop with T-shirts and baseball caps and mugs and posters in the window.

"Now we're talking," said Ruby.

Flora opened her purse and consulted a piece of paper that she had unfolded. On one side was a list of people she needed to buy gifts for. On the other side was her budget. "This could take a while," she announced. "I'll have to shop very, very carefully." When they left the store, Flora had bought a *Lion King* T-shirt for Nikki and a mug featuring the Empire State Building for Olivia.

Ruby had bought nothing.

"I think we're all flagging," commented Min.

"Maybe dinner will revive us," said Allie.

"Dinner?" said Flora and Ruby.

"How about Chinese?" asked Allie. "I know the perfect place."

As soon as they were seated in the Chinese restaurant, Flora decided that *this* was the most exotic spot she had ever been in. The walls were red and gold. A statue of Buddha was peeking over Min's shoulder. The table was set with forks and knives and chopsticks.

"Bird's nest soup," said Ruby, studying the menu. "Is that really made from . . . twigs and dog fur?"

"Here's egg drop soup," said Flora. "You know, they could combine the soups into one dish. Put the eggs in the nests."

Ruby giggled. "Instead of dropping them."

Min said, "I think you girls are getting punchy."

Flora thought that maybe she was a little punchy. But she didn't care. This had been one of the best days of her entire life.

CHAPTER 17

Saturday Evening, November 28ᵗʰ

Ruby might not have tried the snails. And she passed up a great number of things on the menu in the Chinese restaurant on Friday night, finally settling for chicken with cashews, picking all the cashews out and setting them daintily aside on her plate. (The cashews had been cooked and were soft and vaguely slimy.) But on Saturday, she tried something that she couldn't wait to tell her friends in Camden Falls about (her friends no longer including Lacey).

Ruby ate a chestnut.

She didn't want to. Not after Aunt Allie told her the source of the wonderful smell that had reached her nose as she and Min and Allie and Flora once again walked along Fifth Avenue. "What is that?" Ruby asked, breathing in deeply. The air was cold and Ruby was cold and she could see her breath puffing out in front of her as they made their way toward a store called Lord & Taylor that Allie claimed had the best

Christmas windows in the city. "I smell . . . is it pop-corn?" It didn't smell quite like popcorn, but it did smell awfully good. More important, it smelled like it might be warm.

"You smell chestnuts," replied Allie. "Hot chestnuts."

"Gross!" cried Ruby.

"No, really. They're awfully good. In fact, they're a New York treat. You *have* to get roasted chestnuts on a winter day in New York City. Come on. Let's find the cart. It's got to be nearby."

"There it is," said Min.

"I am not eating chestnuts," said Ruby flatly.

"I'll try one," said Flora.

"Show-off," said Ruby.

They approached a two-wheeled cart with smoke rising from the top and disappearing into the frigid air. A man wearing a dusty sweatshirt, a faded wool cap, and the strangest gloves Ruby had ever seen was shoveling hot brown nuts into little bags.

"What happened to his gloves?" Ruby whispered to Min.

"Hush," replied Min. "Nothing. They're fingerless. They keep his hands warm, but he can make change without taking them off."

"Huh. Clever," said Ruby.

Aunt Allie now held out a bag of the chestnuts and Ruby eyed them suspiciously. "They're big," she said.

"You have to peel the shell off," Min told her. "The nut is inside, all hot and toasty."

Flora tentatively reached into the bag and withdrew a nut. Ruby watched her. The shell came off easily, and Flora held the nut, wrinkled and yellowish, in the palm of her hand. "Hmm," she said. Then she glanced at Ruby and popped the entire thing in her mouth. She chewed carefully. "Hey, it's good!" she exclaimed. "It's sort of nutty and popcorny at the same time. Try one, Ruby. Go ahead."

Against her better judgment, Ruby reached into the bag and withdrew a chestnut. She peeled the smooth shell away. "If they wanted people to eat these things," she said, "they should have made them look better."

"Just try it," said Flora.

So Ruby did. "It *is* good!" she said. "Gosh. I should have tried snails after all."

"Maybe they'll be on the menu tonight," said Flora.

"Oh. Yeah," said Ruby, who had forgotten that she would be eating in another restaurant before going to the theatre that night.

When the chestnuts were gone, Ruby and her family made their way to Lord & Taylor, and Ruby saw why her aunt liked their windows.

"These are the best ever!" she exclaimed. "Just like you said, Aunt Allie."

"They're certainly putting me in the Christmas spirit," added Min.

"Just think," said Allie, gazing at Santa Claus and his reindeer-drawn sleigh soaring through a starlit sky, a teeny earth far below, "this Christmas, Janie will be with us."

"Her first Christmas," said Min.

Ruby said nothing. She glanced at her sister, who was also silent, and knew Flora was thinking what Ruby couldn't bring herself to say: that Janie *might* be in Camden Falls for Christmas. Or she might be at home with her birth parents.

They edged past the rest of the windows, pointing and exclaiming and marveling at all the wonderful, fanciful details — an elf's lighted buttons, miniature popcorn strung on an equally miniature tree in a dollhouse, a mechanical cat swatting at a toy mouse. When at last they had inched their way out of the line, they crossed a side street and Allie said, "We'd better go back to the apartment now. We need time to get ready for tonight."

"Yes!" cried Ruby. "Time for Broadway."

Even though Aunt Allie had said that no one got dressed up to go to the theatre anymore, Min had insisted that every one of them put on their very best clothes. "We will not," she said, "attend the theatre looking like a bunch of hobos."

When they left the apartment that evening, Flora and Ruby were wearing velvet dresses, Min was wearing her best going-out-to-dinner suit, complete with a gold necklace that Ruby had never seen before, and Allie was wearing a brocade vest and a pair of black silk pants. Min frowned slightly at the pants, fancy as they were, but said nothing. "A good thing, too," Allie whispered to Ruby. "I didn't pack a dress."

They took a cab back to Midtown.

"Where are we going to have dinner?" asked Ruby as the city sped by outside the windows.

"At one of my favorite restaurants," Allie replied. "Joe Allen. It's near the theatres, and lots of people eat there before shows."

"Famous people?" Ruby wanted to know.

"You might see a famous person or two," Allie replied.

Ruby was excited into speechlessness.

The cab pulled up in front of what looked like a very small restaurant, but when Ruby stepped inside, she found that Joe Allen was larger than it appeared. Fascinated, she examined the walls, which were hung with posters of Broadway shows. Then she noted that over the bar was a television. A football game was playing, but Ruby said breathlessly, "Min, could we ask them to change the channel? I want to see if *Everybody Loves Raymond* is on."

"No TV," Min whispered back.

"Yeah. Let's go see if there are snails on the menu," said Flora.

There weren't, to Ruby's relief. And so she felt comfortable enough to say to the waitress, when it was time to give their orders, "I was hoping to try snails, but I guess tonight's not the night."

"Maybe they have a snail special," said Flora, and Ruby's eyes widened.

The waitress laughed. "You're off the hook," she told Ruby.

Ruby ate a hamburger. She told the waitress about life in Camden Falls. She asked to be alerted if anyone famous came into the restaurant. She examined the posters and imagined her name on all of them: Ruby, child actor. Ruby, tap-dancing queen of Broadway. Ruby, grande dame of stage and screen.

When Min looked at her watch and said that it was time to leave for the theatre, Ruby realized that she hadn't thought of Ms. Angelo or the Children's Chorus or her awful mistake in hours. She let out a sigh of contentment. New York was the place for her.

The theatre was everything Ruby could have hoped for. It was large. It was grand. The seats were red and plush. The curtain, ponderous and sweeping, was also red and was trimmed with gold braid.

"Pinch me," Ruby whispered to Flora as they lowered themselves into their seats. "I'm either dreaming or I'm in heaven."

Flora obligingly pinched her. "Neither," she whispered back. "This is real."

Ruby opened her *Playbill* and read about the actors she would see that night. She hadn't heard of any of them, but that didn't matter.

Ruby was on Broadway.

"Min?" she said. "Can we get popcorn?"

Min smiled. "This isn't like a movie theatre, honey. No popcorn. But at intermission we'll see if we can get a snack."

Ruby blushed. She felt she should know such things. She buried her nose in the *Playbill* and was relieved when at last the lights dimmed. She reached for Flora's hand and squeezed it. "The adventure begins," she whispered.

The orchestra played the overture and Ruby, rapt, watched the conductor waving his baton. But when the curtain rose, Ruby was disappointed. She saw a stage that was bare except for a spotlight. Where was the fancy scenery? She had been hoping for a set loaded with props and backdrops and furniture. But in seconds she found that she didn't care one bit about the set. She became lost in the world of the theatre. Ruby knew the music from *Spotlight*, but since she had never seen a production of the show she was hazy about the story. Now she learned that the play was about putting on a play: about actors and singers and dancers, and their stories and how they had reached this particular point in their lives — what drove them to become performers, and what putting on this play night after night meant to each of them.

Ruby could relate. This world, the world of show business, was hers. She applauded all the talented performers who were working so hard at what they truly loved.

Ruby was thoroughly enjoying herself. She was lost in the stories of the actors, and had already cried a little, when suddenly the story of one actor in particular, Eva, became clear to Ruby. Eva had once been a very famous actress who had won all sorts of awards, but now hardly anyone would hire her, so she had settled for a teensy little part, appearing only briefly as someone's aunt, and wearing, Ruby noted, a very unflattering wig.

Ruby gulped. What had happened to Eva? How had she fallen from grace? Ruby had a sinking feeling that she knew the answers to those questions. She could hear Min's voice as plain as day, telling Ruby that she had become a bit cocky. Was this what happened when people became cocky? Nobody wanted to work with them and their careers began to slip?

Ruby lost track of the story for a while. She pictured herself in her bedroom in the Row House, glancing at the music for the Thanksgiving performance . . . and setting it aside, deciding that she knew it already. She remembered her rash decision not to attend the rehearsal at the end of the first day the Doer of Unpleasant Jobs had been in business. Then she saw herself standing on the risers before half of Camden Falls, not knowing when to begin her solo. Well, at least she *knew* her solo, Ruby said to herself. She knew the music, she knew the words. But she had felt that she didn't need to work with the rest of the chorus, and that had cost her dearly. Now she saw exactly where such an attitude could lead. One day Ruby might wind up as Eva, a washed-up former star, scrambling for lowly roles, settling for work of any kind, just to be able to pay her bills.

Ruby tried to focus on the stage and the performers again. She glued her eyes to Eva. She was not, she told herself firmly, going to become Eva one day. She would not take anything for granted. If she wanted to be a professional (again, she could hear Min's words in her mind) then she would have to work hard. She had a strong suspicion that when Ms. Angelo said Ruby was on probation and could actually be asked to leave the chorus, she meant it.

In the cab on the way back to the apartment that night, Min said, "Ruby, you're awfully quiet."

"I'm thinking about the show."

"Did you enjoy it?"

Had she enjoyed it? "Yes," said Ruby, aware of the trouble Min had gone through to get the tickets.

But she couldn't stop thinking about Eva.

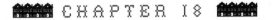

Sunday Morning, November 29th

Nikki was awakened on Sunday morning by Mae pouncing on her in bed and exclaiming, "One more day of vacation!"

Nikki had been thinking about the subject a bit differently. When she had gone to bed the night before, she had said grumpily to herself, "Just one more day of vacation." And then it would be back to school and homework, Tobias would be gone . . .

"Ugh," said Nikki with disgust.

"Nikki! What's the matter with you? We have one more whole free day! Maybe we can make Christmas ornaments. Or — I know! — maybe Tobias will drive us into town. Hey, let's make pancakes for breakfast!"

At last, Nikki smiled. "Okay. Pancakes. I like that idea."

Nikki, with a great deal of sloppy help from Mae, made a pancake breakfast for her family.

"This is heavenly," said Mrs. Sherman as she sipped her coffee later. She glanced uncertainly around the messy kitchen, though.

"Don't worry," said Nikki. "We're going to clean up, too. That's part of the deal."

"It is?" said Mae unhappily.

"Definitely. Mom's been working very hard."

"I'll help," said Tobias. "It'll go fast, Mae. You'll see."

"Thank you," said Mrs. Sherman.

"When we're finished," said Mae, "we're going to make Christmas ornaments." (Nikki had not yet agreed to this.)

"That sounds like fun," said their mother, "but before you get started, I need to talk to you — to all three of you."

Nikki, who had been rinsing off dishes in the sink, turned around and faced her mother warily. "About what?" she asked.

"I'll explain in a few minutes."

"But —"

"Come on," said Tobias, nudging Nikki. "Let's finish up. Mom, where do you want to talk?"

"In the living room."

"Okay." Tobias handed Mae a dish towel. "Nikki's washing," he told her. "You dry, and I'll put things away."

"Tobias, do you know what Mom wants to talk about?" asked Nikki. She could feel the pancakes sitting uncomfortably in her stomach and wished she hadn't eaten so many.

"Nope. But Mom looks serious, so let's finish cleaning up and find out what's going on."

"I have a bad feeling —" Nikki started to say.

Tobias nodded pointedly in Mae's direction. "But it's important to think positively."

Nikki closed her mouth and concentrated on the dishes. When the kitchen was clean, she and Mae and Tobias sat in a row on the couch in the living room, facing their mother, who was perched stiffly in an armchair.

"Mommy, you're not smiling," observed Mae. "So I know this is something bad."

"No," replied Mrs. Sherman gently. "It really isn't. But it is something serious, and we need to discuss it."

"Did someone die?" asked Mae suddenly.

"Good lord, no!" exclaimed her mother. "What made you say that?"

"It was the worst thing I could think of."

"Mae, I just said that it isn't bad. Now, listen, kids. I've wanted to talk to you about this for a while, but I was waiting until we were all together."

"Are we moving?" interrupted Mae.

Mrs. Sherman sat back in her chair. "No!"

Nikki put her arm across her little sister's shoulders and then reached around to clap her hand over her mouth. "Let Mom talk," she said sternly.

"While it isn't bad news," Mrs. Sherman continued,

"I thought you might feel somewhat . . . unsettled. So I waited until the end of vacation to have this discussion. I didn't want to spoil Thanksgiving."

The pancakes in Nikki's stomach gave an ominous lurch.

Mrs. Sherman drew in her breath. "All right. I think you know that your father and I are in touch from time to time," she began. "We've been writing letters and we've spoken on the phone."

Nikki's mouth fell open. She had a horrifying feeling that the next words out of her mother's mouth would be, "And we've decided to get back together." Nikki said nothing, though, and was grateful she had held her tongue, because when her mother went on, she said, "And, well, we've decided to get a divorce."

Up until that very moment, if anyone had asked Nikki how this news would make her feel, she would have replied, "Great. It couldn't happen sooner." But now that the news was staring her in the face, and even after her short-lived fear that her drunken father was going to return to their lives, she found that what she really wanted was a chance to go back in time, a chance to erase the nastiness and retract the words spoken in anger, a chance for her family to start over, or to do whatever you had to do in order to wind up with two happy parents and three happy kids living together under the same roof. Which was sort of silly, because how many families like that did Nikki know? Flora and

Ruby lived with their grandmother, and plenty of other kids at her school lived with just one parent or with foster parents or went back and forth between divorced parents. A mom and a dad and a few kids was hardly a standard family these days. And yet that was exactly what Nikki now found herself wishing for. But she couldn't say any of these things, not in front of Mae, who still believed in fairies and ghosts and might well believe that they could be a happy family if only Nikki wished hard enough.

"I thought you were already divorced," said Mae. "Last year I told everybody in my class that you got divorced."

Mrs. Sherman cleared her throat. "Well, it's true that Daddy doesn't live here anymore, and we don't intend to live together again. But we haven't actually gotten the divorce. We need to sign some papers and see a lawyer to make it official."

"I think this is a good thing," said Tobias after a moment.

Nikki took his thought one silent step further and realized that her brother meant this was a good thing because now their mother would be free to get married again one day.

"It *is* a good thing," said Mrs. Sherman. "At least, it's the right thing. Legally we need to do it. And I'm telling you about it now because in order for this to happen, your father will have to return to Camden Falls soon." Beside her, Nikki felt Tobias stiffen. "We'll see the lawyer together, and your dad will come to the house to pack up the rest of his things."

"Where's he going to live?" asked Mae. "I mean, after the divorce?"

"He isn't sure," said Mrs. Sherman (at this, Tobias jerked his head up sharply), "but I suspect he'll go back to his job. He's working in South Carolina at the moment."

"That's far away, isn't it?" asked Mae nervously.

"Very far away," Mrs. Sherman assured her.

"When is he coming back here?" asked Nikki.

"Probably in January. We want to get this taken care of as soon as possible."

Tobias had edged away from Nikki and now sat forward on the couch, his hands clasped desperately. "Where is he going to stay while he packs up his stuff?" he said roughly.

"Well, he'll have to come to the house in order to do that," replied Mrs. Sherman.

"I know, but where is he going to *stay*?"

Nikki glanced uneasily at her brother. Here was the Tobias from the old days, the one whose temper could erupt in the blink of an eye.

"I don't know," said Mrs. Sherman. "We haven't worked out all the details yet."

"Well, he is not going to stay here," Tobias told her. "I won't let him. He can stop by to pack up his stuff, but that's it. He'll have to stay somewhere else. And I plan to be here when he's in Camden Falls. I don't care when that is. I'll take time off from school if I have to."

"Why, Tobias?" asked Mae, her voice wobbling. "Why do you need to be here?"

Mrs. Sherman glared at Tobias, and he made an effort to relax. "It's not important, Mae," he said. "Don't worry. I just want to see Dad, that's all."

"Mom?" said Nikki. "After you and Dad are officially divorced, will Mae and I have to spend any time with him? That's what other divorced kids do. They live with one parent and visit the other, or they go back and forth between their houses. I know Tobias won't have to do that if he doesn't want to since he's eighteen, but what about Mae and me?"

Before their mother could answer, Mae leaped to her feet. "I don't want to visit Daddy!" she wailed. "I want to stay here."

"Believe me, you're not going to visit Dad," said Tobias, temper boiling again.

"But he might demand that we visit him," said Nikki, who could feel her throat thicken. Tears weren't far away. "What about custody arrangements? He might agree that we can live here during the school year, then he'll get us for the summer and vacations."

"Mommy, no!" cried Mae. "No! I don't want to go far away from you! And I don't want to stay with Daddy."

"Everyone, please calm down," said Mrs. Sherman quietly. She stood up, crossed the room, squeezed between Nikki and Mae on the couch, and slipped her arms around them. "I really don't think that's going to happen. I do not think your father is going to push for custody arrangements like that. He doesn't like responsibility, and I frankly don't think he could afford to support you for an entire summer."

"What about for a week? What if he wanted us at Christmas or for a week in the summer?" said Nikki, and now the tears did begin to fall. "We've never been to South Carolina. And I don't want to live with Dad for even a day."

Mrs. Sherman turned to Nikki, but before she could say anything, Tobias got to his feet. "I wouldn't let that happen," he said. "I wouldn't let any of those things happen."

"But what if the judge said we had to go?" Nikki tried not very successfully to hold back a sob.

"Honey, I think you're getting way ahead of things," said her mother. "I would never have brought this up if I thought you'd get so upset."

"That doesn't help any!" wailed Nikki. "I thought you were going to say you didn't bring this up because these things aren't going to happen and we're worrying for nothing. But you didn't say that. You think they might happen, don't you? And you just don't want us upset."

"Nikki, Nikki." Her mother gathered her in her arms. "Of course I don't know for sure what your father is going to ask for or what a judge might say, but I truly do think you're worrying for nothing. Can you honestly see your father making all the arrangements necessary for you and Mae to visit him? Or having enough money to support the three of you instead of just him? He barely remembers to send us money as it is. And if it came to it, all you'd have to do is tell a judge about the kind of father your dad was when he lived here. I don't think any judge in his right mind — or hers — would decree that you and Mae had to spend time with him far from home. He might be granted visitation rights here, but how often do you think he'd make his way back to Massachusetts? He hasn't been here in almost a year as it is.

"Seriously, Nikki," continued Mrs. Sherman, "set these worries aside. You, too, Tobias and Mae. Let's just concentrate on getting through the divorce. That will have to happen first. And before *that* . . ."

"Yeah?" said Tobias and Nikki.

Mrs. Sherman looked at Mae.

"Before that," said Mae obediently, "comes Christmas."

"Yes. So let's think about having a nice holiday."

"All right." Nikki fumbled for a Kleenex and blew her nose. "But I am not going to let this go. I'm going to read and study about divorces and custody arrangements and visitation rights and I'm going to be prepared if I have to talk to a judge. I'm going to make sure I'm taken seriously."

The rest of the morning passed more quickly than Nikki had thought it would. She did indeed make tree ornaments with Mae, trying to concentrate on pinning and gluing and snipping and coloring instead of on her father. When lunch was over and Tobias said it was time for him to go back to school, Nikki wrapped him in a fierce, tight hug and he held her close.

As he was walking out the door, his laundry bag now full of clean clothes, he whispered to her, "I will *never* let anything happen to you or Mae."

CHAPTER 19

Sunday, November 29ᵗʰ

"I can't believe we have to go home today," were the first words out of Ruby's mouth when she awoke on Sunday morning. She rolled over and peered at her sister, who was sleeping next to her on the sofa bed in the living room.

Flora rolled away from Ruby. "What time is it?" she managed to mumble.

"Six-forty-four," said Ruby brightly.

"*Six-forty-four!* You're never awake this early on a weekend."

"But this isn't just any weekend. It's a weekend in New York City. I don't want to waste a second of it."

"Aren't you tired? We went to bed so late last night."

"Nope," said Ruby. "Not a bit tired." She bounced on the bed. "I hope we can eat breakfast in a restaurant before we go home."

"One last chance to try snails?" muttered Flora from beneath her pillow.

"Ha-ha. No, I saw a big coffee shop a few blocks away. Do you think Min would let us eat there by ourselves?"

"Just you and me? Absolutely not."

"Well, maybe we could at least sit at a separate table and pretend we're by ourselves."

"Ruby," said Flora, assuming a most annoyingly adult tone, "you've hardly mentioned Janie the whole time we've been in New York. Are you only thinking about restaurants and sightseeing and souvenirs? Don't forget the reason for our trip."

"I didn't forget about Janie! But Aunt Allie can't visit her or anything, and I didn't want to make her feel bad. I was thinking to myself, Allie has to go back to Camden Falls today without the baby, and that's very sad. You should really try to put yourself in other people's shoes, Flora, and see things from their, um, from their . . . shoes."

Flora did not reply.

"I'm going to go see if Min and Aunt Allie are awake yet," said Ruby. "I want to ask about the restaurant."

"Go out for breakfast?" was Min's sleepy reply when Ruby jumped on her bed a few moments later.

"Please?" begged Ruby. "I know we have to go home this morning, but we do have to eat breakfast — you always say it's the most important meal of the day —

and if we eat out, then Aunt Allie won't have to cook for us."

"Very thoughtful of you," said Min. "Any particular place you had in mind?"

"The Silver Spoon," replied Ruby instantly. "I saw it on Friday. I think it's only a few blocks from here. It looked like a great place for breakfast. It's very big and has booths and twirling displays of desserts."

"Which you are not going to eat for breakfast."

"No, no, of course not."

"All right. I'll see what Allie wants to do."

An hour and a half later, Ruby, Flora, Min, and Aunt Allie were dressed, their suitcases were packed, and Allie had taken several walks through the apartment, checking to see that she had left everything in order.

"I guess we're ready," she said at last. "We can bring our things downstairs and leave them in the lobby while we're at the restaurant."

And so Ruby bid a sad good-bye to the only Manhattan apartment she had ever known. As she walked out the door she said to herself, Someday I'm going to live in an apartment just like this. Except that it will be in a building full of famous people.

The Silver Spoon was exactly as Ruby had described it. It was indeed very large and full of both tables and booths. And near the cashier's counter by the door were three tall display cases in which cakes, pies, pastries, and even dishes of Jell-O cubes rotated slowly.

"Min?" said Ruby.

"No."

"Darn. Well, if I can't have a dessert, then could Flora and I at least sit at our own table?"

"At your own table?"

"You know, and pretend we're here by ourselves."

Min glanced at Aunt Allie. Then she looked around the restaurant. "I suppose it would be all right," she said at last. "Does this mean you want to pay for yourselves, too?"

"Min!"

"Or better yet, treat all of us," said Allie.

Ruby reluctantly opened her wallet and began to count her money.

"We're teasing, honey," said Min gently. "Yes, you and Flora may sit at a separate table as long as Allie and I can see you. We don't want you far away. And we'll pay for breakfast."

"Thank you! Oh, thank you, Min!" cried Ruby. "Come on, Flora."

Min grabbed her arm. "Wait. The hostess will show you to a table."

As Ruby followed the hostess to a booth by the windows, she decided that she had never in her life felt quite as grown-up as she did at that moment, especially when she realized that some of the other people in the restaurant were watching her. She whispered to Flora,

"Those people are probably thinking, Look at those girls out for breakfast all by themselves. They must be real New Yorkers."

Ruby was slightly disappointed when the hostess then showed Min and Aunt Allie to the very next booth, but she recovered quickly when a waitress arrived at their table and said, "What'll it be, girls?" and didn't even ask what they were doing there without grown-ups.

"This has been the best meal of the whole trip," said Ruby with a satisfied sigh as the waitress cleared their table later. "Don't you feel grown-up, Flora? Don't you feel like you belong here in New York?"

"This has really been fun," said Flora truthfully. She refrained from adding that she was now ready to go back to Camden Falls and King Comma and Daisy Dear and Olivia and Nikki and all her familiar things.

"But you're ready to go home, aren't you?" said Ruby. Flora nodded. "I knew it. Well, I'll be glad to get home, too, I guess. But New York is . . . magic. I wish I could keep it with me always."

After Min and Aunt Allie had helped Ruby and Flora pay their bill and had shown them how to calculate a tip for the waitress, they stepped out into the cold air and sunshine and began the walk back to the apartment building. Halfway there, Ruby suddenly bent down and scooped a handful of grit from the sidewalk.

"Ruby! Ew! What are you doing?" yelped Flora.

"Taking this home."

"That . . . dirt?"

"This isn't just any old dirt. This is a Manhattan souvenir. And it's the best kind."

"Because it's free?" said Flora.

Ruby made a face at her. "No. Because it's a little bit of the Big Apple. I guess you could say it's a little *bite* of the Big Apple."

"What are you going to do with it?"

"Put it in a jar. And keep it on my bookshelf, where I can look at it every day. Does anyone have a baggie?"

Miraculously, Min produced a baggie from her voluminous handbag. "I knew this would come in handy one day," she said.

Ruby emptied the dirt into the baggie and wiped her hands on her jeans, and they made their way back to the apartment building, where they collected their suitcases. In no time, they had piled into Allie's car and were driving north on the West Side Highway, headed for the George Washington Bridge.

"Back to our home," said Flora with a happy sigh.

"Back to reality," said Ruby, who could feel her mood take a nosedive. Flora would be happy enough to return to school the next day, but Ruby didn't feel ready. Furthermore, the thought that she was on probation in the Children's Chorus flew back into her mind, unbidden and unwelcome. That thought was followed by another equally unwelcome one: Her solo in the Christmas concert had been taken away. And it had probably been given to Lacey. How was Ruby going to face her friend?

Soon, Allie's car was speeding along the Palisades Parkway. In the front seat, Min fell asleep. Next to Ruby, Flora fell asleep, too.

"Why don't you take a nap, honey?" called Allie.

But Ruby couldn't sleep. Suddenly, she was overtaken by her poisonous thoughts. Perhaps, she thought, she could arrange for some sort of accident to befall Lacey. What if Lacey broke her arm or twisted her ankle? Better yet, what if she lost her voice? But if Lacey couldn't sing the solo, then Ms. Angelo would just give it to someone else. Ruby would not be singing it. Ms. Angelo had made that clear. Ruby was going to have to work hard to revive her career.

She stared furiously out the window until the scenery began to blur, and eventually she fell asleep after all. When she awoke, it was to the sound of her sister saying, "Good old Main Street."

Ruby opened her eyes. "We're back already?"

"Yes," said Aunt Allie from the driver's seat. "And I'm going to drop you off at the Row Houses and then go on home. Mom, I'll call you later," she said to Min as she turned onto Aiken Avenue.

"Okay. Rudy is going to drive me to the train station in a little while so I can retrieve my car."

And just like that, Thanksgiving was over, the thrilling weekend was over, and New York seemed like a movie Ruby had watched a long, long time ago. She stuck her tongue out in the direction of Lacey's house as she lugged her suitcase up Min's front walk and Allie drove away.

Then Min unlocked the door and several things happened all at once. Daisy Dear came flying down the stairs from the second floor so fast that she stumbled on the fourth step and crash-landed at everyone's feet. King Comma trotted into the front hall and stretched himself against Ruby's legs. And from behind them a deep voice said, "Did you have a good trip?"

"Rudy!" cried Min. "What a nice surprise!" She gave Mr. Pennington a long hug.

"We had the *best* time!" exclaimed Flora.

"We went to Broadway," said Ruby. "And I ate a chestnut."

"We saw the windows at Lord and Taylor," added Min.

"We ate at a French restaurant and a Chinese restaurant," said Flora.

"Come have a cup of tea with me before we leave for the station," said Min to Mr. Pennington, and hand-in-hand they walked toward the kitchen.

Flora dragged her suitcase upstairs.

Ruby was looking forlornly at her bag of dirt when she heard a timid knock at the door. She opened it and found Lacey standing on the stoop. "Hi," said Lacey. "Can I come in?"

Ruby glowered at her. Then she slammed the door shut.

"Ruby Jane Northrop!"

Ruby froze. Min had returned to the hallway. She was reaching for her purse.

"Yeah?" said Ruby.

"Was that Lacey?"

"Yeah."

"Open that door this minute, young lady."

Ruby turned the doorknob. Lacey was crossing into the Malones' yard, one shaky hand rubbing her eyes.

"Lacey," said Min gently. "Come back." She ushered Lacey inside, then took her by one hand and Ruby by the other, led them into the living room, and sat them on the sofa.

"Ruby," said Min, "that was one of the rudest things you have ever done, and I want you to apologize to Lacey right now."

"Sorry," said Ruby.

"You never, ever" (Min continued looking directly into Ruby's eyes) "*ever* slam a door in anyone's face for any reason. Do you understand me? It's humiliating and mean and petty."

"Sorry," said Ruby again.

"I'd like you to imagine how you would feel if someone slammed a door in your face."

Ruby nodded. "Horrible," she said. And added yet again, "Sorry."

"All right. Now, I promised Mr. Pennington a cup of tea, and I expect that you two have some things to discuss. So I'm going to go back into the kitchen and I want you girls to stay here and talk things over. Civilly."

Ruby nodded and Min left the room. "Lacey?" said Ruby. "I really am sorry. I guess I —" She paused, uncertain how to continue. "Ms. Angelo gave you my solo, didn't she?" she said at last.

Lacey nodded. "I knew you'd be mad."

"Well, I am. But not at you. You aren't the one who skipped rehearsals and made a giant mistake during the concert. And anyway, you know you deserve the solo."

"But Ms. Angelo offered it to you first. That must mean she thinks you're better."

"Not necessarily. She tries to give everyone a chance. And I blew mine. But you're not going to. You'll do a great job, Lacey. Doing well at something," said Ruby slowly, "comes partly from being really good at it and partly from working hard. That's what I learned this weekend."

"You learned that in New York?" said Lacey suspiciously.

"Yup. We went to this play on Broadway —"

"On *Broadway*?"

Ruby nodded. "It was called *Spotlight*. And there was this character in it named Eva." Ruby told Lacey about how Eva had fallen out of favor. "So, see, even though Eva was really talented, she couldn't get parts anymore, except for playing maids and old aunts and stuff. Which is what I mean about being good at what you do *and* having to work hard. And that's you, Lacey. You go to all the rehearsals and you practice at home. You work really hard . . . and you have a beautiful voice."

"Thanks," said Lacey quietly. "I *am* excited about singing the solo. I just didn't like getting it this way. And I didn't want you to be upset."

"Well, I'll be sad not to be singing the solo at the concert," admitted Ruby. "It's going to feel weird. But I do have a chance to start over and I'm going to take it seriously. I guess that's why Ms. Angelo put me on probation."

"You're on pro*bat*ion?" squeaked Lacey. "Like a criminal?"

"I prefer to think of myself as an experiment," said Ruby stiffly.

Lacey nodded. "Anyway, are we friends again?"

"Yeah."

"Good." Lacey relaxed. "So, did you get any souvenirs in New York?"

Ruby nodded. "I'll show you the best one," she said, and went off to find her bag of dirt.

CHAPTER 20

December

Flora liked Camden Falls during every season of the year. She liked her town when it put on its spring face and the dull, dreary days of February and March became green and pink and violet and azure, just as if, Flora thought, a giant had taken up his paints and brushes, colored in the town, and added leaves and flowers and freshness. She liked Camden Falls in summer, when school was out and she and her sister and friends planted vegetables and swam in the freezing water at the state park and wandered along Main Street, eating ice-cream cones and watching the tourists. She liked autumn, when the giant's palette changed and the trees burned orange and vermilion and gold and bronze, and pumpkins grinned from porches and Main Street got ready for Halloween night. But her favorite season in Camden Falls was winter. As soon as Thanksgiving was over, Main Street began to glow and glitter with the holiday decorations put up by Mr. Freedly and the owners of the stores and businesses in town. Wreaths appeared on doors. Menorahs appeared in windows. It was the season of lights and of darkness, Flora thought dramatically. The days were short and dim, but it barely mattered because the town twinkled and shone.

And now, miracle of miracles, it was December again, and had been for nearly two weeks. Min and Flora and Ruby had bought a tree, which they had decorated with help from Mr. Pennington, and then they had helped him decorate his tree. Flora's house smelled of pine and cinnamon and peppermint and chocolate. And it was filled with secrets. Ruby had hidden something under her bed, something she refused to discuss with anyone. Min had declared the guest bedroom — the one that, just a year earlier, had been occupied by Aunt Allie — absolutely off-limits to Flora and Ruby.

"Aren't you just dying to peek in there?" Flora whispered to Ruby one evening.

"I already have."

"You *have*?"

"Well . . . I tried to. But it's locked! Min locked the door!"

"*Ruby.*"

"I wonder where the key is. Do you know?"

"No. And it's a good thing I don't. Besides, you wouldn't want someone peeking under your bed, would you?"

Ruby narrowed her eyes. "*Have* you been peeking?"

"Nope. I like to be surprised."

"So where are you hiding *your* stuff?" asked Ruby.

"I'm not even going to give you a hint."

But this year, though it was as exciting as the previous one, was different. Some of the best surprises had nothing at all to do with the holidays and instead were about Jane Marie. Jane Marie was doing well, and so was her mother, and in two days Camden Falls was going to become Janie's home.

A surprise baby shower had been planned for Allie and Janie, to be held on a Thursday afternoon, the moment Allie walked through the door after her final trip to Manhattan.

"Girls?" Min called up the stairs on Wednesday evening. "Are you coming with me to Allie's? We should leave in just a few minutes."

"Coming!" replied Flora and Ruby instantly.

As they clattered down the stairs, Min said, "I want to do as much as possible to get ready tonight, because tomorrow afternoon is going to be busy. Can you give me a hand with the food, please?"

Flora and Ruby helped Min carry bags of party food to their car, and then they drove through the quiet dark streets of Camden Falls toward Allie's house.

"I hope it snows for Christmas," said Ruby wistfully. "I hope we have a big old white Christmas."

"Snow for Christmas would be lovely," said Min, "but not for the shower. And not for Allie's drive back from New York tomorrow with the baby."

"No! We don't want anything to spoil that," said Flora hastily.

When they reached Allie's house, Flora couldn't help taking one more peek at Janie's nursery. Allie had been delighted with the makeshift nursery she had discovered after the Thanksgiving adventure in Manhattan. But since she hadn't been able to bring Janie home with her yet, she had had time to buy a new crib and changing table and to pick out fabric from which Min and Flora had made curtains and a matching crib set.

Flora looked around the room and let out a sigh. The nursery was a cloud of pale pink and blue and yellow. A teddy bear sat in the Morrises' white rocking chair — on a pink cushion made by Flora. Allie had painted the dresser blue with gold stars. It looked, Flora thought, like the ceiling in Grand Central Station. On the wall above the crib hung the word JANIE in jaunty yellow and pink gingham letters.

Still, the room looked a bit bare. The shelves of the bookcase were mostly empty, and so was the top of the dresser.

"And that's exactly why we need to give Allie a shower," Min had said. "She may have bought a lot of baby things, but she still needs a lamp and books and toys and stuffed animals. And, of course, everyone wants to welcome Janie home."

"Allie is going to be so surprised tomorrow," said Flora when she returned to the kitchen to help Min with the food.

"Did you finish your present?" Min asked her.

"Yup," replied Flora, opening a package of paper plates. "But it's all wrapped up. I don't want anyone to see it before the shower."

"I have a good surprise, too," said Ruby.

"And I will have a good surprise," said Min, "if I can get in about an hour of knitting time tonight."

"Oh, I am so excited about tomorrow!" squealed Ruby. "I can't wait, I can't wait, I can't wait!"

"Just imagine — our first peek at Janie," said Flora rapturously. "I wish it were time for the party right now."

To Flora's relief, school flew by the next day, and before she knew it, she and Olivia and Nikki were walking to the Row Houses so Flora could pick up her gift for Janie and they could all drive to Allie's with Min and Ruby.

"What if Allie and Janie get there before we do?" said Ruby nervously from the backseat. "Wouldn't it be awful if we couldn't surprise her?"

But the driveway was empty, and they were able to hurry inside and set out the food before Allie or any of the guests arrived.

"Now remember," Min said later as twenty-eight people sat eagerly in Allie's living room, "this is going to be a very quiet surprise. We don't want to frighten Janie, so no shouting or jumping up and down when Allie walks through the door."

"Okay," said Flora. But she couldn't sit still. She walked nervously among Ruby and Nikki, Olivia and her parents, Mr. Pennington, Robby and his parents and the other Row House neighbors, Gigi, and even Mary Woolsey, until finally Ruby let out a shout:

"They're here! They're here!"

Min opened the door. "Welcome home," she said softly as Aunt Allie carried Janie to the front porch. "We have a surprise for you," she added. She opened the door wide so Allie could see the friends and neighbors gathered inside.

Allie's mouth dropped open and her eyes filled, but she smiled a wavering smile and then put a finger to her lips, pointing at Janie, who was sleeping soundly.

Flora, standing just behind Min, stood on tiptoe for her first glimpse at her new cousin. She gazed at the soft brown face and the finely curled black hair.

Ruby peered at Janie, too.

"What do you think, girls?" asked Aunt Allie.

Flora suddenly found that she wasn't going to be able to speak without crying, and anyway, she didn't want to say something that sounded like a line from a movie ("I've been waiting for Janie all my life," or "Now our family is complete") so she simply stepped forward and kissed the baby lightly on her forehead. And Ruby, parting the blankets to find a small hand, stroked the tiny fingers and whispered, "I don't care if she *is* a girl."

Allie stepped all the way inside then, and Min closed the door behind her. The guests returned to the living room, moving in near silence until Robby said rather loudly, "What are we waiting for? Let's get this party started!"

Now Allie could see the sign that had been strung across the mantelpiece, proclaiming IT'S A GIRL, and the pink and white balloons tied to the backs of chairs, and the unwieldy mound of gifts stacked where, in two days, a Christmas tree would stand. "Oh," she said. "Thank you so much. This is a wonderful surprise."

Everyone began to talk (quietly) all at once.

"How was your drive home? Is Janie a good traveler?"

"I can recommend an excellent pediatrician."

"I wonder if she's sleeping through the night yet."

"Look! The baby just woke up! She's squinting at me!"

Flora began to feel overwhelmed, and as the guests chatted with Allie, and Min held Janie for the first time, and Ruby passed around the cookies and brownies that Olivia's parents had baked, Flora stood back. She watched the party as if she were much smaller than a human girl, as if she were a spider in a corner. She saw Lacey and Alyssa counting the gifts that Allie would soon open. She saw Min pass Janie to Mr. Pennington and settle her on his lap. She saw Robby put out a gentle hand to stop a wrestling match that was about to turn into a fight between Jack Walter and Travis Morris. She saw Mary Woolsey sitting apart from the other guests but smiling, her hands folded lightly in her lap.

And Flora thought, Today is Janie's first day in her new home, but she won't remember it. She won't remember the moment she arrived here and began to make her place in Camden Falls. Janie will grow up here; this will always be her home. She won't be the newcomer, not in the way Ruby and I were once newcomers. She'll belong here from the beginning.

Then Flora thought, This baby, this one tiny baby girl, has transformed our family.

Nikki touched Flora's elbow. "Look how happy your aunt is," she whispered. "I've never seen her like that."

"Me, neither," Flora whispered back.

Allie was smiling — grinning, actually — but she looked serene, too. She radiated peace and calm as Mr. Pennington laid Janie in her arms again.

"When are we going to open the presents?" cried Alyssa Morris, who was standing impatiently over the pile of gifts. "I can't wait any longer."

"They aren't for you, you know," said Travis.

"I don't care! Open them!"

"Flora?" said Aunt Allie. "Would you like to hold Janie while I open the gifts?"

"Hey!" cried Ruby indignantly before Flora could answer.

"You can hold her, too," said Allie. "You and Flora can take turns."

Flora settled herself on the couch next to Allie and held out her arms. Allie placed the baby in them, and for quite a while Flora did little other than gaze at the solemn face peeking out of the blankets. Allie opened present after present, and Flora was aware of a general chorus of "Ooh!" and "Look at that!" and "How cute!" but she couldn't take her eyes off of Janie. Eventually, one tiny fist made its way out of the blankets and waved giddily at Flora. Flora placed her finger in the hand and Janie squeezed it.

"Flora," said Allie suddenly, "this next gift is from you." She peeled away the paper, opened the box inside, and lifted out a blue dress with white rocking horses smocked across the front. "Honey, did you make this?" whispered Allie, and Flora nodded. "It's lovely."

"Thank you."

The dress was passed around, and everyone examined it and exclaimed over it and said it looked professional.

The purple sweater Min had knitted elicited a similar response.

Ruby's gift caused a few eyebrows to furrow. "It's a . . . disappearing quarter trick?" said Aunt Allie.

"The *Wondrous* Disappearing Quarter," said Ruby. "It will be Janie's first magic trick. I got it at Maty's Magic Store."

"That was very thoughtful of you," said Allie.

Ruby was the one holding Janie when she began to fuss.

"Time for a bottle," said Allie.

"We should probably get going," said Robby's mother, "and let you and Janie settle in."

The guests began to leave then, and while Ruby and Min tidied the living room, Flora followed her aunt upstairs to the nursery. Allie placed Janie in her crib, drew the curtains, and turned on a music box. Then she stood over the crib and began to hum softly.

Flora slipped out of the room, intent on helping Min and Ruby with their chores. As she passed the closet in the hallway, she turned the knob and peered inside. The shelves that had once held packages of unused baby items now held half-empty cans of paint, a flashlight, several packages of lightbulbs, a stack of dust rags, and a mop.

It was a very ordinary closet.

CHAPTER 21

A Peek in the Windows

Plenty of tourists visit Camden Falls, Massachusetts, in the summertime, and on certain weekends throughout the year. The weekend before Christmas is an especially busy one, and also an especially festive one, since Camden Falls is wearing its holiday face. Come look at Main Street on this snowy Saturday. A crowd has gathered around the window of Sincerely Yours, where the winners of a gingerbread house contest are displayed. A blue ribbon has been placed before the entry made by the Morris family — the Row Houses with frosted roofs and eight candy wreaths on eight chocolate doors. Robby Edwards stands just inside the entrance to Sincerely Yours holding a tray of cookies and candies. "Free samples!" he calls. "Get your free samples inside."

In the window of Zack's, the hardware store, microwave ovens and toasters and tool kits and reading lamps are displayed among tinsel and greens and tin stars and even a dancing Santa Claus.

Next door is Needle and Thread, and if you wait just a few minutes, you'll see four girls come laughing out of the store, in high spirits because they have decided to finish their Christmas shopping today.

"Mae's the only one left on my list," says one of the girls, Nikki Sherman. "I always save her for last because she's the most fun to buy for."

"What are you going to get her this year?" asks Olivia Walter.

"A jewelry kit," says Nikki instantly. "Or a craft kit of some kind. I can only spend eight dollars, but looking for bargains is part of the fun."

"Let's go to Maty's Magic Store," says Ruby Northrop.

"What on earth are you going to get in there?" asks her sister, Flora, thinking of Janie's bizarre baby present.

Ruby looks at her as though she's crazy. "Magic tricks, what else?"

"I mean, who are you getting magic tricks for?"

Ruby purses her lips. "Let's just say it's a good place to find stocking stuffers."

The girls are in high spirits as they make their way down Main Street. When they reach Sincerely Yours, they help themselves to the free chocolates, calling hello to Olivia's parents and Robby as they dash in and out of the store. Later, they pause to admire the lighted tree in the town square before they cross the street to Maty's.

If you don't mind an outing in the snow on this chilly Saturday, put on your boots and take a walk to a tiny fairy-tale cottage not far from Main Street. This is the home of Mary Woolsey, and on this morning she's looking eagerly through her mail. She has just received a packet of photographs from her newfound sister, and now she sees her and her brother and their children and even their grandchildren. Her hands shake slightly as she reads the note that accompanies the photos, the one confirming that in four weeks she and her sister will actually meet. Mary will open her door and, at her advanced age, greet her sister for the first time. Mary shakes her head in wonder.

Now follow the county route to the outskirts of town. Take a left on a rutted lane, and at the end of it you'll find a shabby but cheerful house with a small girl and a large dog playing in the yard.

"You be a reindeer," Mae Sherman says to Paw-Paw, "and pretend to pull my sleigh. I promise I won't be mean to you like the Grinch was when he made his dog put on reindeer antlers." Mae amuses herself for a while, but something is on her mind and eventually she leads Paw-Paw indoors. "Mommy?" she calls.

"In the kitchen," replies Mrs. Sherman.

Mae removes her boots and mittens and coat and stands by the refrigerator.

"Is something wrong, honey?" asks her mother.

"How many days until Daddy comes back?"

Her mother pulls out a chair and sits down, holding her arms out to Mae. "Is that really what's on your mind?" she asks as Mae slides onto her lap. "I thought you were going to ask how many days until Christmas."

"I know how many days until Christmas. But I wish Daddy was coming first so we could get that over with. That would be my best Christmas present."

Her mother holds her close.

Several miles away, Mr. Willet is preparing for his first Christmas at Three Oaks. He stands in his small living room and surveys his decorations. He's not entirely pleased. The tree in the corner is fake, since evergreens are fire hazards and not allowed anywhere at Three Oaks. And he gave many of his decorations away before he moved. The ones he's left with are lovely, mostly heirlooms from his family and from Mary Lou's, but the room looks nothing like his old living room in the Row Houses, and he sinks onto the couch. But then he rises again and decides to take the flower arrangement that arrived that day from Min and Mr. Pennington downstairs to Mary Lou. It will brighten her room.

If you were to head back into Camden Falls now, you would reach Main Street as the day darkens and people begin to close their shops and hurry home. Turn onto Aiken Avenue and ahead are the Row Houses, lights winking on in the windows. In the

Morrises' house on the left end, the children are still exclaiming over their first-prize ribbon.

"We won!" cries Travis.

"I never won anything before," says Alyssa, awed. "Never in my life."

Next door, the Hamiltons have parked in front of their house and Mr. Hamilton is struggling up the walk, dragging a Christmas tree behind him.

"Our first tree and our first Christmas in our new house," says Willow.

Nobody mentions that Mrs. Hamilton won't be home for the holiday.

In other houses, cookies are coming out of ovens and gifts are being wrapped and cards are being displayed on mantels. In the fourth house from the left, Ruby is once again trying the door to the locked guest room. She still can't open it and she still hasn't discovered where Min hid the key. In the second house from the right, Robby has returned from his job, and he and his parents are wrapping a bagful of toys that they'll take to the children's shelter on Monday. In the house at the right end, the Fongs are getting ready for Grace's first Christmas.

And not far away, a new mother and her new baby are rocking quietly in a chair beside a fire. The mother strokes the baby's black curls and rocks and rocks and hums a lullaby while the fire crackles and outside the darkness becomes complete and the stars glow in the night sky.